THREE GO TO THE CHALET SCHOOL

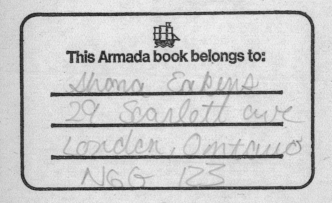

First published in the U.K. in 1948 by
W. & R. Chambers Ltd., London and Edinburgh.
This edition was first published in Armada in 1979 by
Fontana Paperbacks,
14 St. James's Place, London SW1A 1PS.

This impression 1981.

© W. & R. Chambers 1948.

Printed in Great Britain by
Love & Malcomson Ltd.,
Brighton Road, Redhill, Surrey.

THREE GO TO THE CHALET SCHOOL

Elinor M. Brent-Dyer

Armada

CONTENTS

CHAPTER ONE

MARY-LOU AND CLEM

'BUT *why* mustn't I' demanded Mary-Lou, standing very straight and square, her blue eyes looking levelly at Mother and Gran.

'Because your mother says you mustn't,' retorted Gran with her usual crispness.

Mary-Lou glanced a little more steadily at her, but said nothing. That was the kind of remark you expected from Gran. She was a dear, and kind, and an absolute rock when you were in real trouble; but she did think such queer things about obedience, and tidiness, and keeping yourself 'like a young lady, and not a young hooligan.' Mother was not half so strict, thought Mary-Lou, who – at the age of nine, nearly ten – would have ruled her mother with a rod of iron had it not been for Gran. The old lady saw to it that her small grand-daughter was brought up in the way she should go. So, after that one steady look, Mary-Lou turned to her mother and waited for what was to come.

'Oh, dear!' began Mother in worried tones. 'I don't think Clem and Tony are quite the right kind of friends for you, Mary-Lou.'

'But they *are* my friends,' Mary-Lou stated simply. 'I can't *not* be friends with them, Mother. We've been friends since they came to Polquenel. Why aren't they the right sort now when they were at first?'

Silence! Mrs. Trelawney really felt unable to explain to her small daughter that it was not so much Clem and Tony to whom she objected. Admittedly their various activities were death and ruination to Mary-Lou's clothes, and from a quiet little puss she had turned into a regular tom-boy since they had become such chums, learning to climb the cliffs and rocks, and turn cartwheels, and whistle with such shrill effect that Gran declared it went through her head like a knife. The real trouble lay with their parents, Mr. and Mrs. Barras, and especially Mr. Barras. He was an artist with a wonderful flow of language when he was aroused – which happened at least once a day, and frequently oftener. Mrs. Barras was a pretty, feather-headed woman, who seemed to think that as long as her children were more or less clothed and fed, and had beds to sleep in, and went to school fairly regularly, she had done her full duty by them.

When they had first come to the big bungalow next door to Tanquen, the Trelawneys' house, Mother had made no objection to Mary-Lou being friendly with eleven-year-old Clem and the three years younger Tony. Indeed she had been very glad to learn that children so near her little girl's age had come next door, for it was rather lonely for Mary-Lou at Polquenel. Thus the friendship had been smiled on by everyone.

It was rather more than a month later before. Mother and Gran could call on Mrs. Barras. The day after her arrival, Mother began one of the colds that seemed to be coming more and more frequently this past year or so, and it had been impossible to call till she was well again. Then they had gone, and found Mrs. Barras in a soiled and paint-stained overall, with hair looking as if it had not been combed for a week – Mrs. Barras had a bad habit of running her fingers through it when she was perplexed or worried. The room into which they were ushered by Clem, who happened to be in the house, was equally untidy, with dust lying *in layers*, as Gran said later, and nothing in its place, while the mistress was curled up on the window-seat, making a pastel-study of the view from the window. And this at half-past three in the afternoon!

Even then, nothing had been said. Mary-Lou, an only child, considered too young to take the ten miles' bus-ride to Melion, the nearest town, for school, doing lessons at home instead, had rejoiced in her new friendships, and the three had become inseparable out of school-hours.

That had been a year ago, and as time passed it was borne in on Mother and Gran that Clem and Tony were a pair of wild young scaramouches. They were fast turning Mary-Lou from the quiet, old-fashioned little maid she had been, into something as wild as themselves. But what had really brought about the present situation was that Gran had chanced to overhear Mr. Barras giving the butcher a piece of his mind that morning, and had been shocked almost to swooning-point by his language. They had often heard roars of fury from the bungalow, and on one occasion Clem had created quite a sensation in Tanquen, where she and Tony had been invited to tea, by observing casually when an especially noisy rage was heard, 'There's Dad going off the deep end again. I wonder what it's about *this* time?'

Gran had been uneasy then, and had contrived to infect Mother slightly with her disquiet; but they had left it till that morning, when the elder Mrs. Trelawney had marched into the drawing-room on her return from the village with the awful tale of Mr. Barras's remarks to poor Pengelly.

'This friendship must *cease*!' she had wound up. 'Heavens knows what that child may have picked up! I suppose, Doris, you don't want your daughter to learn that kind of language at her age?'

Most emphatically Mother did *not*! Hence, when lunch was over, and just as Mary-Lou was rushing off to join Clem and Tony for a joyous afternoon in the cove, she had been called back and asked where she was going. And on hearing, Mother had told her gently that she preferred her to be less friendly with the Barras children in future.

Mary-Lou stood there now in a patch of sunlight which turned her short fair plaits to gold, and lay lovingly on her round tan-and-rosy face. Her brief blue gingham frock was faded and a good deal too short, Gran thought, for the girl was growing fast just now. Her sturdy bare feet were in shabby sandals which had been too small for

7

her, but the resourceful Clem had cut the heels and toes open with her father's razor – the storm following his discovery of this had been devastating! – so that Mary-Lou could still wear them, sandals being difficult to get in their part of the world, and Mary-Lou objecting strenuously to giving up the dear shabby things that fitted every little kink of her feet so comfortably.

Mother looked at her, and her eyes softened. But Gran was watching – Gran, who saw to it that if Mary-Lou were an only child, at least she was not spoiled – and she spoke.

'In any case, Mary-Lou, you won't have much more time with them.'

'Why not?' demanded her grand-daughter quietly.

'Because we are leaving Polquenel for good shortly.'

'Leaving Polquenel? – But – but it's *Home!*' Mary-Lou looked bewildered.

'Not after six weeks or so more,' returned Gran firmly. 'We are going to live some distance away from here. There isn't a decent school near enough for you to go to, and it's too bleak for your mother in the winter. We're going to a place where it's warmer. It's not far from a really excellent school where you will go every day.'

Mary-Lou was silent for a moment or two. Gran had taken the wind out of her sails this time, and she wasn't very sure what to think. To gain time, she asked, 'What's "bleak", Gran?'

'Cold and unpleasant,' answered the old lady briefly. 'Every winter lately your mother has had one cold on top of another. She needs to go somewhere where we don't get those awful west winds sweeping right across the ocean from October to April – or even later. We've found such a place, and in six weeks' time we shall pack up and be off.'

'For always, do you mean?' Mary-Lou sounded dazed She *felt* dazed. Her whole short life had been spent in Polquenel, with perhaps five or six weeks every summer at some holiday resort. She couldn't imagine living anywhere else.

'For the next few years, anyway,' amended Gran. 'If this place suits your mother we shall probably live there until you finish with school, at least; say till you are seventeen or eighteen. It all depends.'

'But,' Mary-Lou did a hasty sum in her head, 'that's *eight years!* I shall be *old* then! Do you mean we aren't coming back to Polquenel for eight whole years, Gran?'

'Probably. Oh, we shall come back for a short holiday sometimes, I expect,' said Gran, softening a little under the horrified blue gaze of her small grand-daughter. 'But we shan't *live* here.'

'But – our house? It's ours. How can we leave it?' protested Mary-Lou.

'No; it's not our house,' replied Gran. 'It never was. It belongs to Mr. Brownlow at St. Asaph's Lodge. We have paid rent for it while we've lived in it – you know what that means, don't you? – but it isn't ours.'

Mary-Lou nodded. 'Of course I know what rent is. It's what you pay someone for letting you have the house. But I didn't know we paid Mr. Brownlow. I – I thought it was ours.'

'Well, now you know it isn't. He wants it for a friend of his; and the doctor says your mother ought not to live here any longer, or she'll have a cold once too often; so we're leaving it. Now do you understand?'

'I – I see.' Mary-Lou stood for a minute longer, digging the cut-off toe of her sandal into the thick rug on which she stood. Then she turned and made for the door.

'Where are you going?' asked Gran.

'Down to the cove – to Clem and Tony,' said Mary-Lou. 'I – I promised them I would, Gran. I *must* go!' And she took to her heels and fled.

'Do you think she need have been told yet?' asked Mother, when the last flutter of her daughter's brief skirt had vanished behind the flowering shrubs that bordered the path.

'She had to be told sometime, hadn't she?' demanded Gran. 'It would have been a bigger shock to her if we'd done as you suggested, and left it till the vans were at the door for the furniture. She knows now, and will have time to take it in. But we must try to break off this friendship, Doris. She seems to have a perfect craze for those two young imps next door! Well, no doubt time and absence will do it. Now I'm going to sit down and make up the housekeeping books for the week; and you had better go and take your rest. You know what the doctor said. Don't worry about Mary-Lou. *She'll* be all right.'

Meanwhile Mary-Lou was flying at full speed down the sandy village street to the cove, saying over and over again in her mind, 'We're going right away! We shan't come back for years and years! I shall be *awfully* old – quite grown-up – when we come back again! How simply *dreadful*!'

She turned the corner between two rock-built cottages with fuchsias growing up to the very roofs, covering the walls, and scrambled down the rocky footpath that led down to the cove where Clem and Tony were waiting for her. They were rolling on the sand like a pair of puppies, but something made them look up, and they jumped to their feet, waving to her.

'Come on, Mary-Lou!' shouted Clem. 'What an age you've been!'

Mary-Lou covered the last part of the journey in a series of goatlike leaps that landed her almost on top of them, drawing from Tony a protest of 'Here! Look out, you moke! That was nearly me!'

'Sorry!' gasped Mary-Lou, who was out of breath with her haste.

'What's up?' demanded Clem, her quick eyes seeing more agitation in Mary-Lou's face than was warranted by her nearly jumping on top of Tony – an almost everyday occurrence.

Mary-Lou's words tumbled out at such a rate that it was a minute or two before they could make out what she meant. 'We're going away – leaving Polquenel! I've never lived anywhere else in my life! We shan't come back till

10

I'm ever so old – eighteen, anyhow! And *that's* old! Gran said it!'

Clem's eyes, warm reddy-brown like the thick elf-locks that tumbled over her shoulders to her waist, widened. 'But what on earth is there in that to upset you? *Good night!* I've lived in a dozen different places at least; so has Tony. We never stay long anywhere. Why, we're leaving here in another two months' time or so. Dad said so at dinner to-day.'

'You're leaving too?' Mary-Lou dropped down on the sand and mopped her hot face with the skirt of her frock, as she had lost her handkerchief, 'Do you really mean it?'

'Of course; we've been here as long as we've been in most places, and a lot longer than some,' replied Clem, squatting beside her. 'Dad says he's got all out of here that he's likely to get and we'd better move on. I think,' she added, 'that it was those awful sausages yesterday that did it. They went all queer when Mums cooked them. You never saw such a sight! Dad was just raging! This morning he went down to tell Pengelly just what he thought of them and him – or so he said. But I don't think he did it, 'cos he came home with a ducky little sketch of the Mermaidens' rocks. But he was simply mad last night, for there wasn't another thing in the house but bread and cheese, and he likes a decent meal at night does Dad. Oh, there *was* a barney, I can tell you!'

'I heard it. My bedroom window was wide open,' said Mary-Lou briefly.

'I'll bet you did! If Dad really went to Pengelly's and said all he meant to, I should think the old thing's foaming at the mouth. It'll be too bad, for he may decide not to serve us any more, and then poor Mums will have to go somewhere in Melion for meat.'

'Dad never thinks of things like that when he's in a real tearing temper,' said Tony cheerfully. 'Anyhow, Mums need only go once to fix it up. We can call for the meat, so that will be all right. Don't worry about Mum's, Clem.'

As so often before, Mary-Lou was left gasping at the

way they spoke of their parents. Sometimes, it seemed to her, they behaved almost as if *they* were the father and mother, and Mr. and Mrs. Barras were their children. Never in all her life had she even thought of taking care of Mother, though she was always ready to run errands and wait on her if she were told to do. But Clem and Tony saw things and did them without being told.

Tony flopped down beside the girls. He was a thin, long little boy, with the same red-brown eyes as his sister, and a shock of fair hair at present in much need of cutting. Mary-Lou had sometimes felt dimly that if Gran and Mother had had charge of Clem, she might have been very pretty; but Tony was a plain little boy, burnt sallow by the sun, and with a wide sensitive mouth under a nose that the politest person could have called nothing but 'snub'. Both children wore zebra-striped jerseys in blue and white, and blue shorts. Clem's hair was supposed to be tied back with a ribbon to match her stripes, but she had lost it during their morning games, and had tied her hair back with one of her father's shoe-laces.

Tony turned over on his face, and began to scrabble in the sand as he spoke. 'You've been here a jolly long time, Mary-Lou. It'll be rather fun for you to see a new place. I like seeing new places myself.'

'But I've *always* lived here,' said Mary-Lou rather piteously.

'Time you got out and lived somewhere else for a change, then,' said Clem. 'Any idea where you're going?'

'No – only that it's somewhere where we won't get the west winds and Mother won't catch colds. Oh, and there's a school for me to go to. I don't want to go to school. I'd heaps rather go on having lessons with Mother and Gran. I've never been to school; and I don't like girls.'

'You like me – I'm a girl,' said Clem.

'Ye-es; but you're not awfully like other girls – not if those girls that came to the Vicarage the summer before you came are ordinary girls,' said Mary-Lou resentfully. 'I loathed *them* all right! Horrid like pigs! And they spent all their time saying things like, "Don't you know *that*? Haven't you seen this? How *quaint* of you!" I'm not quaint, and I didn't like them one bit! I just hate thinking of going to school!'

Clem grinned broadly. She and Tony knew all about 'the Vicarage girls'. Their father had come to Polquenel as locum tenens while Mr. Charteris, the Vicar, went for a long and much-needed rest. His name was Simpson, and his two girls, Anne and Margaret, had been thirteen and eight respectively. Mother and Gran had rejoiced in the thought that for three months Mary-Lou would have a chance of girl-friends more or less her own age; but it hadn't worked out like that.

Anne and Margaret had been gently patronizing, and Mary-Lou had resented it fiercely. They had behaved beautifully to each other when any grown-ups were about; but left alone they had quarrelled bitterly. The day came when Mary-Lou invited to tea at the Vicarage, had left the garden incontinently before she had been there an hour, and had flatly refused to return either then or at any other time. It is true that Mrs. Simpson, by dint of sharp questioning, had found out what was wrong, and after scolding her own pair severely and threatening them with a governess for the rest of the holiday if they did not mend their ways, had brought them to Tanquen to apologize. It made no difference to Mary-Lou, who had been left feeling that if the Simpsons were fair samples of girls who lived in a town, she didn't want to know any more.

Mary-Lou saw Clem's grin and it infuriated her. 'Stop grinning at me like an ape!' she cried. 'You wouldn't have liked them yourself!'

'I shouldn't; but then they wouldn't have tried it on with me – or only once, anyhow,' said Clem calmly. 'Don't get your rag out, Mary-Lou. From all you say, I should think they were a pair of hopeless little ninnies. All girls aren't like that, you know. Anyhow, you'll have to go to school some time, and the earlier you get it over, the easier it'll be.'

'I don't see why I must,' said Mary-Lou, still resentfully. 'Mother and Gran could go on teaching me. They know heaps more than I do.'

'Wasn't your mother at school?' asked Clem.

'Yes, but the Head died and the school ended, or she'd have sent me there. She's often said so. I mightn't have minded that. It sounds fun when she talks of it.'

'I don't suppose you'll dislike your own school when you do get there,' said Clem shrewdly. 'After all, your mother and Gran are very decent. You might trust them to be able to choose a decent school for you.'

'But – but it's so *sudden!*' complained Mary-Lou. 'And oh, Clem, they both say I mustn't be so friendly with you two, and I don't see *why!*'

'I can guess.' Clem sat up, looking grave. 'I saw your Gran going into Pengelly's this morning, and if she was there when Dad landed and heard him get going – well, you know what he is. She needn't be afraid he'll say anything in front of you, though. He's awfully careful what he says when you're there. *We're* accustomed to him, so he doesn't mind us much. But he once said it would be a shame to teach you anything of that kind — Oh, my stars and stripes!' She broke off, and sprang to her feet as a bellow sounded from the top of the cliff. 'What on earth has gone wrong *now?*' She shaded her eyes with her hand, looking upwards to where a big man in artist's smock and flapping trousers was standing, shaking his fist and thundering incoherently.

Tony rolled over, chuckling ecstatically. 'He's found it – he's found it! Oh, I say! Isn't he in a bait!'

'Tony!' Clem swung round on her brother. 'What have you been up to now?'

'I found his touring-box, and I filled it with those tiny crabs and jelly-fish we caught yesterday. Oh, just listen to him!' And he wriggled with mirth.

'He's coming down,' announced Mary-Lou a little apprehensively.

Tony stopped laughing and looked up quickly, but the

14

sun was in his eyes. 'Has he a strap or a cane with him?' he asked rather anxiously.

Clem, her eyes still shielded by her hand, shook her head. 'He's got nothing. He's only roaring and shaking his fist. Tony, you *are* a little ape! If he'd been able to find either you'd have caught it good and hot, my lad. But I hid them yesterday at the back of my clothes cupboard. But I expect you can prepare for a jolly good spanking.'

Tony got to his feet and straightened himself, setting his lips. He had turned a little pale under his tan. When Mr. Barras was really angry, he spared neither tongue nor arm. His small son had known there would be serious trouble over this latest prank, but at the time it had seemed too good fun to miss.

By this time, Mr. Barras had reached the cove and came striding over the sand. His bush of red-brown hair was literally bristling with rage, and his brown eyes were flashing ominously as he reached the little group demanding, 'Who did it? Who messed up my best box like that, eh?'

'I did it, Dad.' Tony spoke up stoutly, but there was a look of fear in his eyes, and his lips were trembling despite all his efforts.

'You did, did you, you – you little *gosling* you!' Furious as the artist was, his eyes had noted Mary-Lou standing beside his children, and he kept firmly to his resolve not to teach her anything undesirable. But oh! just let him get Master Tony away from the girls, and he would teach that young man an unforgettable lesson to let other people's things alone!

Clem spoke up. 'Mary-Lou and I caught the things, Dad. Tony only put them in your box.'

' "*Only* put them in the box!" I like your – your impudence!' her father thundered. 'It's spoilt – ruined! A box that cost me Heaven knows what!'

'Oh, no; it isn't,' said Clem quickly. 'I'll come and clean it out for you, and it'll be all right in half no time. Tony *is* an ass, but it was only a joke.'

15

' "Only a joke!" ' Mr. Barras seemed to choke on the words.

'Yes; only a joke. You've said yourself that a man who can't see a joke, even if it's against himself, should have a – a major operation performed on his skull,' retorted Clem dauntlessly. 'I've heard you say it dozens of times myself. You come back to the house with me, Dad, and I'll clean the box in half a sec. Crabs and jelly-fish aren't dirty things, anyway. And the box is a mess with paint and fixative as it is, so I don't know why you're growling.'

The artist calmed down. 'You're a clever girl, Clemency, my child,' he informed her. 'All right, young man. Your sister's saved you the father and mother of a flogging. But just you listen to me. One more such "joke" of yours, and you're for it – both of you! You'll go straight to the first boarding-schools I can find to take the pair of you.' He glanced round at Mary-Lou. 'Here, young woman! Can you take a message for me?'

'What is it?' asked Mary-Lou, giving him one of her straight looks.

'Tell your grandmother that I'm sorry I forgot myself before a lady this morning. But you can also say that Pengelly's sausages deserve all I said to him and more.'

'We never buy them in hot weather,' Mary-Lou informed him. 'Pengelly hasn't got a – a fridge, and they don't keep. He couldn't have one, anyway, he says, not with no gas and no 'lectricity to work it.'

The artist raised clenched fists to Heaven. 'What a place! What a *hole* of a place! However I've contrived to exist here as long as I have done, I *don't* know! We'll up stakes and make tracks for somewhere civilized!'

'You said that at dinner,' Clem reminded him.

'So I did. Well, I mean it. I'll go back and tell your mother to get to work this very afternoon. We leave here at the end of the week, or my name's not Miles Barras!' And with this he turned about and strode off.

The three stood looking after the enraged artist. 'Oh, bother him!' said Clem at last. 'And bother you, Tony,

16

my lad! If you hadn't done such a daft thing, we'd have been able to get packed and off in some sort of peace. Now it'll be a most fearful scrimmage. I suppose I'd better go up and see if Mums wants me to give a hand. Mary-Lou, you and Tony stay here and play till tea-time, and give him a chance to cool off properly. When he's really mad, he loses his head.' And she ran off after her father, leaving the other two not quite sure what to say or do.

Finally Mary-Lou spoke. 'If you're leaving in a week, we'd better do something now,' she said. 'Let's paddle, shall we?'

'May as well,' agreed Tony. 'Goodness knows where we'll go from here. But it *may* be where there's no sea.'

They paddled accordingly, and Clem, rejoining them an hour later with the information that her mother had gone on a sketching expedition, so nothing could be done for the moment, showed a basket she had filled hurriedly.

'We'll stay here till bed-time,' she said. 'No use giving Dad a chance to remember about you, Tony. I've brought enough for tea and supper for all of us. Can you stay, Mary-Lou?'

Mary-Lou decided that she could; and did. It was seven before she could give Mr. Barras's message, which was received with fair graciousness. No one had worried about her. Gran had strolled to the top of the cliff when she had finished her books and seen where they were. But the fiat had gone forth. Mother and Gran managed to keep her so busy that she saw very little indeed of Clem and Tony for the rest of the week. Saturday saw the furniture-van at the gate of the bungalow, and when the two Barrases came in at eleven that morning to say good-bye, they announced that they were going to London for a few weeks first. From there it would probably be Scotland. 'The Hebrides, Dad talks about,' said Clem. 'He never has been there, and he thinks there ought to be some good subjects. It'll be the *sea*, anyhow, though it won't be like *this* sea. Where we'll go when he's done there, I don't know. See you some time or other, I hope, Mary-Lou.'

Under the eye of Mother and Gran, Mary-Lou gulped down her grief at this offhand leave-taking, and said good-bye. In the midst of all her woe she contrived to note that she had been right on one point. Clem, dressed for the journey in a clean green cotton frock, with her hair neatly brushed and plaited in two plaits tied with dark green ribbons, a big straw hat on her head, her long, scratched legs in neat brown shoes and stockings, was surprisingly pretty. Tony wore a grey flannel suit and a clean shirt and blue tie, and looked like any other little boy, since he had been sent to the barber's in Melion the day before to have his hair cut.

Just as he shook hands he leaned forward – Clem was saying good-bye to Mother and Gran, with very proper thanks for all their kindness – and whispered, 'Buck up, you moke! It'll come out all right in the end. Bet you we meet again jolly soon!'

Then they left, and Mary-Lou, watching the taxi which had come to take them to Melion to get the train right out of sight, finally she ran back into Tanquen mysteriously comforted and ready to look forward much more happily to their own flitting.

CHAPTER TWO

VERITY-ANN

ON the same day that Mary-Lou had it broken to her that the family were leaving Polquenel, another small girl was also facing a complete change in her life.

Verity-Ann Carey stood in the study of the big Rectory. in a Yorkshire village, looking at her grandfather's lawyer with solemn eyes of deepest gentian-blue, and he, looking back at her, was moved to wonder how this child would respond to modern school-life.

She wore a little grey frock that was quite up-to-date in style, but even so, you felt somehow that Verity-Ann herself was a product of at least fifty years ago, with long golden hair falling in masses of ringlets about her shoulders and down to her waist. She had a tiny pale, pointed face, with exquisitely modelled little features, and the said eyes were heavily fringed with long upcurling lashes of brown that gave them a starry look which frequently misled strangers into thinking her a most heavenly minded child. Verity-Ann's manners matched her dress, and her language outdid both, for she had been the companion of two old people, and her late governess was also verging on the mid-seventies.

Mr. James was the father of two girls himself, but he was completely floored by this specimen of girlhood.

Verity-Ann stood before him, hands behind her back, and said in a tiny, silvery voice, 'You sent for me, Mr. James?'

He held out his hand. 'Quite right; I did. Come and sit on my knee while I tell you a few things.'

'Thank you. If I may, I would rather sit on a chair,' she informed him, walking sedately to a near-by chair, where she sat down, hands in her lap, feet side by side.

Feeling rather snubbed, Mr. James did his best. 'Well, now, my dear, I expect you had been wondering what is going to happen to you, now that your grandfather – er – um —'

'Now that Grandpapa is dead, I know I must leave here,' Verity-Ann told him gravely. 'There will be a new Rector, of course, and he will want this house himself.'

'Ah; I am glad you realize that,' Mr. James replied, very much as he would have spoken to her grandfather himself. 'Then you must go elsewhere, and as we can't get in touch with your father at present, it has been decided to send you to school.'

Verity-Ann suddenly flushed. 'Is it necessary?' she asked.

'I am afraid so, my dear.'

'But why? I do not think I should like school.'

'Oh, you'll like it very well once you are there,' he said. Then he added with real curiosity, 'What did you expect to do?'

'I thought perhaps as you are my guardian I should live in your house and have another governess.'

He shook his head. 'Unfortunately, there wouldn't be room. We live in a flat, and in any case it is in London, and London isn't a good place for small people who have been accustomed to the Yorkshire moors. Besides,' he added, 'it's time you went to school. You're ten, aren't you?'

'I was ten last month,' said Verity-Ann.

'Then quite time. My girls were sent away at ten, to the school where you are going. You'll like it there. Joan and Pamela were very happy at the Chalet School.'

'Indeed?' said Verity-Ann politely.

A silence fell. Poor Mr. James felt he really did *not* know how to deal with this self-possessed little person.

'Hang it! She might be forty-odd!' he thought to himself. He stood up. 'Well, I've told you what's going to happen, and I expect you'll be very happy once you have reached the Chalet School. You will have any number of other girls of your age to play with, for one thing.'

'I do not approve of most modern children,' Verity-Ann told him priggishly. 'They are frequently rude and forward, talk slang, and are disobedient and unladylike.'

Mr. James nearly gasped. 'Upon my word!' he exclaimed. 'I think it is more than high time you went to school – if only to teach you to think and talk like a little girl instead of an elderly maiden aunt! Now say no more, Verity-Ann. To school you go, and the sooner the better!'

Verity-Ann cast him a look of bitter dislike. 'I know I must do as you say,' she said in a choked voice. 'But I promise you I will *never* become like one of those modern schoolgirls! I will always talk as I have done, and think so too. I hate this school of yours, and I'll leave it the first moment I can! So there!'

Then, having forgotten for once to behave like 'a little lady,' she turned and fled from the room, leaving Mr. James to pull out a handkerchief and mop his brow. He had had some awkward interviews in his life, but never had he been through one he was more thankful to end.

As for Verity-Ann, having flung down the gage, she rushed away to the garden to a little summer-house which was her own special cubby-hole, and there she threw herself down on the seat, tossed her arms across the little rustic table, and cried stormily till she could cry no more. Then she sat back and began to think things over.

Go to school she must. She recognized that. But she would remember everything she had been taught at the Rectory, and utterly refuse to change in any one way. She had no intention of making friends as Mr. James had suggested. And directly her father came home she would beg him – *implore* him to remove her, and let her live with him and a governess in some pretty house. Perhaps dear Miss Graham could be persuaded to come and live with them.

Up to this moment, Verity-Ann had felt only a tepid affection for the elderly lady who had been responsible for her education, but now she loved her warmly. *Dear* Miss Graham! For a few minutes, Verity-Ann forgot her troubles in a day-dream in which she and her almost unknown father lived in a charming rose-covered house, with Miss Graham to keep house for them and teach herself.

However, this soon passed, and she sat filled with resentment as she recalled her present guardian's last speech to her. No one had *ever* talked to her like that before! How dared he? Just as if she were a naughty, tiresome child, forsooth! Verity-Ann had a great idea of personal dignity, and Mr. James had offended her bitterly. When the tea-bell rang and she had to go back to the Rectory, she went with head held high, and the iciness of her manner was only excelled by her talk.

21

Mr. James recognized ruefully that he had made an enemy. He could only hope that the Chalet School would contrive to convert the girl from her present distaste for modern girls and education.

He left after tea, for he had another client in the neighbourhood to visit, but he saw the old nurse who had cared for Verity-Anne's physical well-being all her life, and bade her have the child ready by two o'clock the next afternoon, when he would take her with him, first to the London flat in which he and his wife lived, now that Joan was married and Pamela in Paris, where she acted as interpreter at the British Embassy, and then to Joan's house at Exmouth, that young lady lady having offered to take the child for the summer holidays so that her parents might not forgo their annual trip to St. Andrews.

'Miss Verity-Ann is all packed up, sir,' replied Nurse primly. 'She will be ready as you say.'

'Good! The men from the storage place will be along on Wednesday of next week. I'll come down to see that everything is all right, but you and the rest can carry on till then. By the way, if there are any of the child's possessions she would like to have with her, put them into a case, and I'll take them back with me when I come again. We can't do much more until we hear from Commander Carey, and Heaven knows when that will be. Soon, I hope!'

Nurse nodded. 'Very well, sir. Then I'll see to it.' Suddenly she paused. Mr. James looked at her keenly.

'What is it, Nurse?' he asked.

'Mr. Roland, sir – it's a very long time since anything was heard of him. The master was saying so the day before he died. I suppose — ' Nurse stopped short, but the lawyer recognized the anxiety in her eyes.

'It's impossible to say anything as yet,' he replied cautiously. 'I went to the Admiralty last week, but they could tell me nothing new. Last November, however, everyone on the Expedition was quite well and safe. We must remember that it is right up-country in a very wild part, and there may be considerable difficulties about getting any news through.'

'Thank you, sir. Then, will that be all?'

'Everything, I think. Later on,' he added kindly, 'I hope you will be able to see something of the child in the holidays. By the way, I've told her about going to school. I'm afraid she doesn't like the idea very much. Perhaps you could manage to reconcile her a little.'

'I'll do my best, I'm sure,' Nurse replied. And that was the end of that. Mr. James drove off in his car, and the Rectory was left with plenty to gossip over.

Verity-Ann was very much on her dignity. Nurse quickly realized that it was little use saying anything to her about school, and gave it up after her first well-meant remarks had been received with a very chilly 'Thank you, Nurse, but I had rather not discuss the matter any more.'

'It's to be hoped they learn you a bit different when you get there, my lady,' she thought grimly to herself as she sorted out her small charge's most beloved possessions, once Verity-Ann had been put to bed. 'I've always said you ought to have a bit more companionship than you had, but the Rector, bless him, couldn't see it. But you've got to live in this world somehow, and you'll have a bad time of it later if you're let go on as you're doing.'

Next morning, she broke to Verity-Ann the news that Mr. James would be taking her away after lunch, and Verity-Ann, who had got up in the same dignified mood as she had gone to bed, heard it without remark. She ate breakfast in almost complete silence. Then she disappeared into the sunny, summery garden, and was gone most of the morning. But when the big school-bell rang out from the village at noon, she returned to the house. There Nurse saw her into a fresh dress, and brushed out with an inward sigh the long silky curls which were her pride. Doubtless this was the last time. She drew them back in the old-fashioned round-comb in which they were worn, gave last turns to the ends of the golden ringlets, and then bade the child to come to dinner.

23

Mr. James was there on time, but his little ward was not less prompt. When the car drew up before the Rectory door she was ready, and climbed into the front seat beside her guardian after saying goodbye to the old servants who gathered to see the last of her. The door was shut once the luggage was safely stowed, Mr. James nodded farewell to Nurse, and then they were off.

And if Mary-Lou in far-away Cornwall looked forward to school with a certain dread, Verity-Ann travelling from Yorkshire to London by car for the first time in her life, thought of it with a bitter resentment that only school itself could hope to efface.

CHAPTER THREE

THROUGH THE HOLE IN THE HEDGE

It was after lunch, and Mary-Lou was standing in the garden at the new home, looking irresolutely round her. They had been at Howells village for two days now, and already the house, Carn Beg, was beginning to look more like home. It was almost a week since they had left Polquenel, but to Mary-Lou it seemed more like a month. Mother and Gran had been busy all the morning arranging things here and there, dusting and polishing furniture, washing china and putting it away, and attending to the thousand and one details that follow any removal. The only break had been when Gran had gone to the village shops and had taken the small girl with her; and that hadn't taken very long.

To Mary-Lou's eyes, Howells was almost a town. Polquenel had been such a tiny place, with just Pengelly's butcher-shop and the little post-office-cum-general-store which old Mrs. Coombes had kept. But here there was 'Parry's,' as most people still called it, though Mrs. Parry had left the shop more than four years ago to go and keep house for her son and look after his two motherless babies, Gladys and Evan. Then there was a butcher called Prosser at one end of the village, and another called Hughes at the other. A little way from Parry's was a small 'all-sorts' shop, and 'Mrs. Jenkyns' where you could buy various articles of drapery and haberdashery, as well as the newest numbers of divers magazines and daily papers. 'Mrs. Jenkyns' also had a 'liberry' consisting of about two hundred novels, mostly the worse for wear, any of which you could borrow for twopence a week. Two of the big banks had a room in a house in which they ran branches, for Howells had a big sheep and cattle market once a week, and someone came out from Armiford, the near-by cathedral town, twice a week to attend to business.

It had all been so new that Mary-Lou had quite enjoyed herself. But after lunch Gran had told Mother she was looking tired and ordered her off to bed. Mary-Lou was told in Gran's firmest voice to go into the garden till tea-time, once Mother had been tucked up and left to rest, and forbidden to go into the village.

'It was different at Polquenel where everyone knew us,' said Gran. 'Here, not a soul does yet; so you'd better keep to the orchard and the garden for the next few days. Now run along; I'm busy.'

Mary-Lou had 'run along' as she was bidden, but she felt very rebellious. There wasn't a soul to talk to, and she was bored. If only she had had Clem and Tony to play with, it might have been good fun exploring the long garden which ran back and front of the house, and the orchard which lay behind the back garden. Doing it by oneself was a poor affair.

The garden, to her mind, compared very unfavourably with the one at Tanquen. There, Mother and Gran, born gardeners both, had, through the years, planted a delightful shrubbery of flowering bushes, which led to a rock-garden where all sorts of exciting flowers flourished. A tiny spring bubbling up in one corner had been persuaded

25

to produce an equally tiny stream which wound in and out, and along its banks they had planted iris, forget-me-nots, and lady-fern. There were two great old trees that had withstood the bitter westerly gales, and between them had hung a glorious swing. There was no swing here. Mary-Lou, in her present disgruntled state, doubted very much if there could be even *one* tree from which the said swing could be hung in this place.

Well, she couldn't spend the whole afternoon just standing about on the front lawn! Perhaps she had better go and take a look at the orchard. That, at least, would be something new. They had had wall fruit trees in Polquenel; but those same bitter winds which had caught Mother's chest so badly were death to most fruit trees. So, though the high red-brick walls of the back garden at Tanquen had given them a William pear and a morello cherry, there had been no orchard. Mary-Lou tossed back the short bright plaits which reached just below her shoulders, and turned and marched round the house to the back garden.

She liked this better than the front, where there was just a lawn with a wide flower border down the two sides, a thick screen of flowering bushes, and two wide, crescent-shaped beds full of roses under the windows. Here, the ground widened as it ran away from the house, and there was a tennis-lawn across the end, though it was running rather ragged now, having been neglected for two months. The small girl raced across it, and came to a may hedge with a little wicket gate through which she passed into the kitchen garden. Here, the gardener, whom they had taken over with the house, was hard at work, 'lifting' potatoes. At the far end were rows of scarlet runner beans; and there were lines of young sprouts, celery trenches, and winter lettuce. At one side there was a row of bush-tomatoes on which the scarlet fruit glowed, red for gathering. One or two gnarled apple trees were here, and Mary-Lou could see rosy-cheeked apples peeping through the leaves on one of them. She went to it, and stood looking up.

'Not much good for eatin', them ain't,' said a man's voice behind her. 'Them's cookers, them is. Likely they'd give yer a stummick-ache. But you come alonger me into the orchard, an I'll pick yer two or three as'll do yer no 'arm.'

Mary-Lou turned to see the gardener. He was a tall, gaunt old man, with kindly eyes as blue as her own, and he was beckoning to her to follow him through a second wicket gate in to the orchard. He wasn't Clem or Tony, but at least he was someone to talk to. Mary-Lou ran after him, and tucked a chubby brown hand into his work-hardened palm.

'I just love apples,' she informed him. 'Ooo-ooh! What a lot! Are all these ours?'

'Aye, Missy; I reckon they are. Now just you wait. This 'ere's a Worcester pippin. Don't see many on 'em these days, but they're a good eatin' apple they are. 'Ere y'are, Missy. What'll yer put 'em into? Aint' no basket 'ere.'

'My skirt.' Mary-Lou picked up the hem of her brief frock to form a bag. 'This'll do, won't it?'

' 'Ere y'are, then. Now, come this way. This 'ere'es a Worcester pearmain. There's them as says it's a disapp'intin' apple, but I reckon you'll like 'em all right. 'Ere!' Another couple joined the pippins in her skirt. 'An 'ere's a Devonshire Quarrenden. There's a couple o' them for yer. Now ye've enough for one time, an' I must get on with my work or them taters 'ull never get lifted. Don't you go an' eat 'em all at once, though, or you'll be bad to-night.' And with this final warning he left her. At the gate he turned and shouted, 'Now, you mind what I says, Missy. Don't eat *all* on 'em 's afternoon, or ye'll be gettin' a dose of castor oil or gregory, most like. Keep the main on 'em for another day. I ain't much time to pick for yer most days.' Then, his conscience relieved, he went back to his work; and Mary-Lou, her skirt clutched to her, wandered about, examining the trees and noting the goodly crop of apples and pears a number of them bore. Some were quite bare of fruit, and there was no one to tell her that

27

these were plums and damsons which had been picked earlier. But she found a big sturdy tree which looked as if it would take her swing quite nicely, for it had a good, equally stout branch which sprang from just the right height. So *that* was all right!

There was no spring to be converted into a dear little stream, but before she had gone very far, Mary-Lou found a delightful mossy-stoned well. 'Found' is scarcely the right word. If the lid had been off, she would certainly have gone head-first into it, for she was peeping at her apples and never noticed where she was going till she fell over the curb. She bruised one knee and bumped both elbows, and her apples rolled all over the place as she fell. She scrambled to her feet and gave the next few minutes to picking them up while she fought with her tears. Then she tried to relieve her feelings by kicking at the well. But the stones were hard, and her sandals toeless, so that she hurt herself a good deal more than she hurt the stones. She sat down with a flounce at last, and began to lay her apples in a row in front of her.

How pretty they were in the green grass! She felt sure that they would taste as good as they looked. Which should she eat first? She picked up a pearmain, and set her small white teeth firmly into it. Mary-Lou was no connoisseur, and she enjoyed that apple. She threw the core into the hedge, and chose a Quarrenden. When that was disposed of, she looked at them again. She was not a greedy child. Moreover, she knew that she was never allowed more than two apples at once. Besides, though castor oil meant nothing to her, she had, on one horrid occasion when she had eaten too many ripe plums, been dosed with gregory by Gran, whose methods were on the Spartan side. Never would Mary-Lou forget that horrible experience, and she had no wish to have it repeated. She would have enjoyed a third apple, but she thought perhaps it would be better not. She piled up the remainder of her treasure in a corner by the well, and set off to explore further.

The well was at one end of the orchard where a hedge

28

separated it from a big meadow. By dint of sundry crouchings and peerings, Mary-Lou at last found a chink through which she could see into it, and her quick eyes caught the gleam of sunlight on water. She pushed hard at two tough stems and got them apart, making a good peep-hole for herself. At the same time there came the sound of gay voices. She broke off two or three twigs and widened her outlook. Now she discovered that there was a good-sized pond near-by, with alders growing in clumps round it, and a big old poplar tree at the far side. Coming across the meadow to this pond was quite a party, headed by three little girls of about seven or eight, armed with shrimping-nets and glass jars. After them trotted a sturdy, fair-haired boy of four or so, driven in reins by a smaller one who was as dark as he was fair. Last of all was a plump young woman with masses of flaxen plaits twisted round and round her head, and a stocking in her hand at which she was knitting swiftly.

The whole party came to the sunny side of the pond, which was just beyond the hedge where Mary-Lou was crouching, and the young woman, spreading a rug that she had carried over her arm, sat down. The three little girls squatted beside her for a moment to whip off their sandals, and then stood up to tuck their frocks into their matching knickers. The boys discarded their sandals too, and then the whole troop made for the water with wild yells of delight.

'Not too far, meine Jüngling,' warned the young woman.

'We'll be careful,' called one of the little girls with a toss of thick chestnut hair from her little tanned face. 'Come on, Con and Margot! Bet you I catch more than you do!'

'Bet you you don't!' screamed another whose hair was, as Mary-Lou had noted, a warm golden. The third was black-haired, but they were very much alike for all that, plainly of one family.

'Not quarrel,' said the nurse firmly. 'Charles, mein Vöglein, come to thy Anna and let her turn up the trousers

29

from the water. Stephen – ah, das its gut!' For the elder boy was tucking up his short trousers as far as they would go. Little Charles came obediently and let Anna roll his up; then he too was off, and splashing joyously in the cool water.

This was too much for Mary-Lou. She broke off more twigs till she had got a wider space cleared. Then she began to wriggle, and first her bright head, then her blue shoulders, and lastly her brown legs went through the hole in the hedge at the cost of a few scratches and a long rip in her frock. Still, she got through, and as the party startled at the sound of her struggles, turned to look, she scrambled to her feet triumphantly.

'It's the new girl from Carn Beg!' cried the golden-haired damsel. 'Mamma said there was one – she saw her with the old lady in Parry's this morning when she went to order the sugar.'

Anna, who had dropped her knitting and got to her feet, spoke with a pleasant smile. 'You are ze Mädchen from Carn Beg?' she asked with a strong foreign accent.

Mary-Lou looked doubtful. What did 'Mädchen' mean?

The dark girl spoke up. 'Anna means, aren't you from Carn Beg?' she said prettily. 'Mamma said she saw you this morning, and she was sure you must be. We were awfully pleased, 'cos there's never been any children at Carn Beg before.'

'Only old Mrs. Pitt, who was about a hundred,' put in her sister. 'What's your name? How old are you? Can you stay and play with us for a while?'

'I'm Mary-Lou Trelawney, and I'm ten,' said Mary-Lou. 'I can stay all right, thank you. Gran told me to come out and play for the afternoon as she's busy and Mother's tired so she's gone to rest. What's your names, and how old are *you*?'

Recognizing that the child was likely to be welcomed as a playfellow for her own charges, Anna sat down again and took up her knitting, and the children came out of the pond and began to make friends with each other.

'Mary-Lou? What a jolly name!' said the chestnut-haired little girl. 'We're the Maynards. These are my sisters, Con and Margot; and the boys are Stephen and Charles. I'm Len.'

'We three are triplets,' added dark-haired Con.

'What's that?' demanded Mary-Lou, to whom the word was new.

'We all came together,' explained Len. 'It doesn't often happen in a family, so Mamma and Papa are very proud to have us like that. We're eight – nearly. Stephen is five, and Charles is just four. We've got a new little brother, but he's at Plas Gwyn – that's our house – having a nap, and Mamma stayed to look after him. His name is Michael. He only came five months ago, so he's still rather new. Have *you* any brothers or sisters?'

Mary-Lou shook her head. 'No; there's just me.'

'When's your birthday?' asked Margot. 'Ours is November.'

'The end of June – the thirtieth. What day's your birth-day?'

'The fifth – Bonfire Night. Mamma once said we were her big bang,' said Len with a chuckle.

'What did she mean?' asked Mary-Lou curiously.

'Why, just that three of us was a surprise. *That* was when we lived in Guernsey. But we don't remember it,' said Len. 'We were just wee babies when we came to live here, and all the boys was borned here, too. Stephen's birthday is Feb'ry, and Charles is June like you.'

'Only yours is at the very end, and his is the very be-ginning,' added Margot. 'I've heard Papa say he had a near shave of being a May kitten.' She finished with an infectious chuckle.

'I'm a June wose,' put in Charles himself. 'Mamma said so.'

'Why do you call your mother "Mamma"?' asked Mary-Lou curiously. 'I thought no one did now. Gran did when she was a little girl, but Daddy called her "Mother", and so do I Mother.'

31

'Mamma liked it better than "Mummy",' explained Con. 'And when you're just little, Mother and Father are hard to say. So they're Papa and Mamma. Very nice, *I* think. I don't like being like everybody, though all our cousins say Mummy and Daddy.'

'I see,' said Mary-Lou – not really seeing at all. 'What do you catch in the pond? Shrimps – or jelly-fish?'

'Neither, of course; this isn't the sea. It's tiddlers,' said Len. 'We don't get them very often though. Let's go and try now. Take off your sandals and give them to Anna to look after, and stick your frock into your knickers in case you get the edges wet. You can have first go with my net if you like. Here you are!' And she put the net into Mary-Lou's hand.

Mary-Lou shook her head. 'Oh, no; it's yours,' she said quickly.

But Len laughed. 'You take it first. Con or Margot will let me have a go with one of theirs presently. We've got to share with Steve and Charles, anyhow, 'cos there are only three nets. Steve broke his when we were at the sea-side, and Charles's got left behind somewhere or other.'

Thus reassured, Mary-Lou kicked off her sandals, took the net, and in a moment would have been splashing riotously in the pond, but an outcry from Anna prevented her.

'But the little dress, mein Vöglein! Come here, and Anna will tuck it into the knickers. There!' as Mary-Lou meekly went to be tucked up. 'So – and so! Now all is safe. Run and enjoy thyself – but go not too far, for it grows deep.'

'How queerly Anna talks,' said Mary-Lou to Len as they splashed about, dredging with the nets, and bringing up mud, weed, and an occasional water-spider, but – alas! – no tiddlers.

'She's Tirolean; that's why,' said Len. 'Mamma and Papa used to live in Tirol when Mamma was young. Only when the Germans came, they all had to leave. Anna came

32

too, and when Mamma married Papa, she went to be their servant. Now she's our nurse, and we love her ever so, all of us.'

'She seems awfully bossy.'

'Not really. But she knows Mamma expects her to keep us from getting in too much of a mess, and as you're playing with us, I expect she feels she ought to look after you too.'

Knowing that Gran would have plenty to say about the rent in her frock as it was, and would certainly have scolded even more severely if she turned up wet and muddy, Mary-Lou said no more. But the fear had not escaped Anna's vigilant eye, and when the young lady gave up the net to Len, she was called to the rug, bidden slip off the frock and sit down, and Anna produced a little pocket-hussif filled with needles all threaded with different colours in sewing-silk and cotton. She quickly matched up the blue frock, and had it finely repaired in a few minutes. Greatly impressed, Mary-Lou said 'Thank you' as prettily as she knew how, and Anna, with an indulgent smile, bade her remember to be more careful another time, and then turned to tell Margot to give her net to Stephen, who had not had a turn yet, though Con had already handed hers to Charles.

Margot was not at all willing to do so. She clung to the handle desperately, and was on the verge of going into a screaming rage, when she glanced up, caught her younger brother's eye, and subsided, handing over the net quite meekly.

That was the only contretemps in a delightful afternoon. Mary-Lou forgot to miss Clem and Tony as she waded about with the others at the edge of the pond, shrieking with them over their captures; or, later on, sitting curled up on the rug between Len and Con, listening to one of Anna's delightful tales about fairies and Kobolds. Stephen, when it was ended, calmly remarked that it wasn't true, anyhow.

'It's a *story*,' remarked Len severely. 'You can't always

33

have stories about things that really happen, Steve Maynard.'

'I like them best,' said Steve bluntly.

'Another day, *mein Kind*,' remarked Anna, 'it shall be a true story, and thy Anna will tell thee about her brother Hansi, and how she went with him to gather wild strawberries on the mountainside, and came back with a baby kid instead,' she added consolingly.

'Oh, tell's now,' pleaded Margot.

But the distant sound of a cowbell ringing brought an end to the afternoon. Len jumped up, exclaiming, 'That's for tea! Here's your sandals, Charles. I'll help you fasten them.'

'Oh, *must* you go now?' asked Mary-Lou disconsolately.

'Oh, yes. When Mamma rings we've got to go at once,' said Con, who was struggling with a sandal buckle. 'Don't *you* have to do as you're told at once? We always do, else its disobeying, and Mamma says that's one of the naughtiest things we can do.'

Mary-Lou, who was an adept at coaxing when she wanted her own way, stared at this. Gran had fits of being particular about obedience, but Mother could be 'wangled' more often than not if Gran were nowhere about. However, she changed the subject and said, 'Well, can you come again to-morrow?'

Len shook her head. ' 'Fraid not. To-morrow we're going to the Round House to spend the day with Auntie Madge and our cousins, 'cos Uncle Jem had gone away to Edinburgh and she wants Mamma to keep her company.'

Mary-Lou had already heard of this beloved aunt and the four cousins, David, Sybil, Josette, and Ailie. She had also heard of the big school where all the girls went which belonged to the same aunt, though she did not teach in it. And she had heard of 'Auntie Rob' and 'Auntie Daisy' who weren't real aunts at all, but lived at Plas Gwyn when they weren't away.

34

'Oh, I wish you could come,' she said mournfully. 'It's so lonely by myself.'

'Best come to school with us, then,' advised Con, standing up. 'Heaps of girls there. You wouldn't be lonely then.'

'I *am* going to school. That's one reason why we came to live here. But I don't know if it's *your* school.'

'Sure to be,' said Len. 'There isn't any other near 'cept the village school; and you won't go *there*.'

The bell rang again, more imperatively this time, and the party picked up its nets and jars, said good-bye, and then struck off across the field, Margot shouting a promise of being back on Thursday, and Con shrieking more advice about joining them at school when it began the following week.

When they had gone, Mary-Lou turned to solve the problem of how she was going to get back to her own premises. Warned by what had happened to her frock before, she decided against going through the hedge again, and had almost made up her mind to disobey Gran and climb over the gate farther along the hedge and come up the road when she was saved by the appearance of Preece, the gardener, coming to put his tools away in the shed at the bottom of the orchard. He quickly put a ladder over the hedge, climbed over himself, and lifted the small girl across. Mary-Lou resolved to ask permission to use the gate another afternoon, even as she thanked him politely. He might not be there another time. Then she ran to rescue her apples before starting for the house.

Gran met her at the side door. 'Where in the world have you been all this time?' she demanded. 'We called you to tea half an hour ago.'

'I was in the orchard first,' explained Mary-Lou, 'and the gardener gave me some apples – look, Gran! I ate two of them, but that was all.'

'Just as well for you. You may have two a day for the present, but no more, Mary-Lou. You'll be going to school soon, and I don't want any bilious attacks to cope with before that, I can tell you. Come along and make yourself fit for tea.'

'Yes, Gran,' said Mary-Lou. Then she gave a little skip that nearly sent the apples rolling over the lawn again. 'Oh, Gran, I've had such a lovely afternoon! There's a meadow at the bottom of the orchard with a pond in it. Some children came to play with their nurse, and I played with them. Their father is a doctor, and they live at Plas Gwyn, that big white house you can see down the lane farther up the road. There are six of them, but the baby wasn't there, of course. Only Len and Con and Margot and Stephen and Charles. Their nurse comes from Tirol, and she speaks so funnily. And what do you think, Gran? Len and Con and Margot are *really* triplets!'

CHAPTER FOUR

SCHOOL!

FOUR days later, Mary-Lou learned that it was to be what she insisted on calling 'The Maynards' Auntie Madge's school.' She had been spending a joyous afternoon in the meadow with her new friends, Gran having given permission quite graciously. The day after that first meeting, a note had come from Mrs. Maynard, asking that Mary-Lou might play in the meadow with her own quintette, and promising that Anna would keep an eye on the small girl. She apologized for being unable to call for the moment, pleading in excuse the work needed to get three girls ready for school. Her new son, too, was one person's work, and she begged Mrs. Trelawney and her daughter-in-law to waive ceremony and come to tea with Mary-Lou on the Saturday. Gran, after a conference with Mother, accepted, and Mary-Lou looked forward to a delightful time with the little Maynards while Mother and Gran were having a grown-up chat with Mrs. Maynard. Especially did she want to see Baby Michael and, perhaps, to be allowed to hold him herself for a little. Len and Con had both assured her that their mother would be certain to say yes.

Mother called Mary-Lou into the drawing-room when she came in. 'Mary-Lou! Is that you, dear? Come here! Gran and I want you.'

Mary-Lou went in and stood in front of them as they sat together in the wide window-seat. 'I'm not frightfully tidy,' she apologized.

'Never mind that for once,' said Gran. 'We've got some news for you.'

'Oh, what is it, please?'

'You're going to school next week, darling,' said Mother.

'O-oh!' Mary-Lou dragged it out. Then she paused. 'P'r'aps it won't be too bad after all,' she said at length.

'Of course it won't be bad,' said Mother with a tender little laugh. 'You funny girl, Mary-Lou! I believe you'd rather go on having lessons alone with Gran and me.'

'Well, it's more 'sclusive, isn't it?' said Mary-Lou gravely.

'A great deal too exclusive in my opinion!' said Gran. 'It is more than time that you were with girls of your own age. You talk as if you were ninety! Exclusive, indeed!'

'Don't you want to know which school it is, dear?' asked Mother.

'Yes, please,' said Mary-Lou, and waited. Then she suddenly added, 'I hope it isn't that funny little school at the Gables right up the valley. Primula Venables says it's a very poor affair.'

Primula was 'Auntie' Daisy's younger – very much younger – sister. But she was nearly fourteen, therefore a 'big' girl in Mary-Lou's eyes, though no one would have been more surprised to hear it than shy Primula, if anyone had said so.

'Indeed no,' said Gran emphatically. 'We told you at Polquenel that you were to go to a big school, and we meant it. This has over two hundred girls, and a very good reputation into the bargain. It is the Chalet School, about three miles from here — '

'But that's the Maynards' Auntie Madge's school!' interrupted Mary-Lou. 'That's where Len and Con and Margot go, and so does Primula. Mrs. Maynard was there herself; and so was their Auntie Rob and Auntie Daisy. It's a *very* good school!'

'I'm glad to hear you approve of it,' said Gran ironically. 'It's a great relief to my mind.'

Mary-Lou ignored her, and turned to Mother. 'Am I really going there?'

'Yes, dear,' said Mother. 'That is one reason why we came to live here. And now, I have an invitation for you for Monday. Lady Russell has invited you to go with the Maynards to the Round House for the day so that you may get to know her girls Sybil and Josette, who also go there – naturally. Josette is about your age, and she thinks it would be nice for you to know someone else who is likely to be in the same form. The Maynards are only Second Form, you know, and the B division of that, Mrs. Maynard told me when I saw her this morning. You will probably be a form or two ahead of them. You'll be glad to know Josette when you get to the school.'

'I'll wait till I've met her,' said Mary-Lou aloofly.

'Mary-Lou! You really are the – the *limit*!' cried Gran, descending to slang in her exasperation. 'Oh, well, if the Russell girls are anything like their cousins, you ought to like them well enough. Now go and make yourself fit to be seen. You look as if someone had been dragging you through a hedge backwards at the moment!'

'We've been practising walking on our hands,' explained Mary-Lou, escaping to her bedroom before Gran could air her views on walking on the hands for girls.

The two tea-parties, however, proved to be all the heart could wish. But Mrs. Maynard was a complete shock. Mary-Lou had expected her to be something like Mother –gentle, quiet and – well – *motherly*! When they reached

Plas Gwyn, however, they were greeted by a tall, dark lady with a delightful smile, who whirled them off to the nursery to see Baby Michael, and then dismissed the small fry to the garden to play till teatime while she entertained Mother and Gran. But after tea – which was a good one – when the two ladies rose to leave, she begged that Mary-Lou might stay till bed-time, promising that someone would see her across the meadow; and then, consigning her baby to Anna's care, came out and played hide-and-seek all over the garden with them, conducting herself as if she were little older than – say Clem! She could beat them all at tree-climbing, and she could run like a hare. Mary-Lou had decided in her own small mind that she looked years and years young than Mother, who was rather quiet and staid in her ways and certainly never climbed trees or ran races with her small daughter. But Mrs. Maynard was like a schoolgirl let loose, and they had twice as much fun as usual.

On Monday, she found that Lady Russell was much more like Mother, though she had expected that, for she knew that she was a good many years older than her sister. But Sybil and Josette were wild scamps, Sybil being a little younger than her cousin Primula Venables, and Josette nearly Mary-Lou's own age. There were also sixteen-year-old Peggy Bettany, and her sister Bride, nearly fifteen, who were also cousins; and Peggy explained that she had a twin brother, Rix. But he and David, the only boy in the Russell family, were spending the last week of their holidays with a schoolfellow. Mary-Lou felt in great awe of Peggy, who would be Upper Fifth when school began, and probably a sub-prefect – whatever that might be – and altogether a very important person, so the others informed her.

From their chatter she learned that there was another Bettany boy named Jackie, who was also away for the holidays, and a twin brother and sister, in Australia at the present, who were just nine. They, and Mr. and Mrs. Bettany, were coming to England next spring, and Maeve and Maurice would probably join the party at the Round

House, for Mr. Bettany – Uncle Dick – was in the Forestry Department in India, and Mrs. Bettany – Auntie Mollie – always went with him.

'What lots and lots of cousins you have!' she exclaimed to Josette and the Triplets when the elder girls had gone off on some ploy of their own. 'I haven't any at all.'

'What a shame!' said Josette, a very pretty little girl with black hair, pink cheeks, and eyes as blue as Mary-Lou's own. 'Haven't your aunts and uncles any children at all?'

'Haven't any aunts and uncles, either,' said Mary-Lou in as offhand a manner as she could assume. 'Father's brother was killed in the war, and Mother never had any. Gran says I am the only one of – of the – the rising generation in our family.'

'Well, never mind! You can share ours,' said Len quickly. 'Mamma and Auntie Madge will be aunties to you, and Papa and Uncle Jem will be your uncles, so you'll be all right after all.'

And when they went in, she calmly informed her mother and aunt that they had arranged for Mary-Lou to call them 'Auntie' because she had none of her own.

'By all means,' said Mrs. Maynard cordially. 'Begin at once, Mary-Lou. I've any number of unofficial nieces, and can always welcome one more. What do you say, Madge?'

Sweet-faced Lady Russell laughed. 'I quite agree, Joey. And I'm sure Jack and Jem will be delighted to have another. So that's settled, Mary-Lou. And now, what about tea?'

When the great day came, Mary-Lou got up in double-quick time for once. With eager fingers she dressed herself in her school uniform of cream blouse with flame-coloured tie, brown tunic with its beautifully cut flared skirt, and brown blazer with the school crest and motto embroidered on the breast pocket in flame. Her pigtails were tied with brown ribbons, and her shoes and stockings were brown too. She looked a real little schoolgirl as she ran downstairs to breakfast, and when Mother kissed her good morning, that lady gave a quick little sigh, for this was the last of her baby.

After breakfast, Mary-Lou put on the big brown velour hat with the school hatband, and pulled on her gloves. She was ready! It was a beautiful September day, and there was no need of the topcoat which she would wear when the colder weather came. Then she and Mother and Gran walked up the road to the little lane at the far end of which stood Plas Gwyn, and a moment later they saw the Morris Ten coming along, Mrs. Maynard at the wheel, and Len beside her, while Con and Margot were sitting in the back with Stephen, who was to join the Kindergarten next summer.

As she drew up, the lady leaned out, calling, 'Hello, everyone! Prim and the twins went off last night as they are to be full boarders this term. I've only the small fry here. Come along, Mary-Lou! Jump in! We don't want to be late the first morning. Got your satchel? That's right! In you get, then!'

Mary-Lou kissed Mother and Gran, and scrambled into the car. Then they were off. Joey Maynard guessed how Mother, at any rate, was feeling, and she thought it kinder to get the good-byes over as quickly as possible. Mary-Lou was far too excited to be upset; but Mother knew that when her little girl came back at night, it would be a new Mary-Lou.

Along the broad highroad they went, turning in at heavy iron gates which Mary-Lou already knew by sight – the Triplets had seen to that. A long avenue, with meadows on either side, then another pair of gates, and they were rolling past a great lawn dotted with clumps of trees, under which, as Con informed her, they did lessons on hot summer days. At the end stood the great mansion where the school was housed, with a terrace round it, and semi-circular steps leading up to the terrace. Mrs. Maynard drew up before the steps, bundled them all out, and led them up to the front door, informing the new girl that on most occasions she would use the side door. She led them

41

into a spacious hall, which had statues here and there, and plants and bowls of flowers set on the tables and window-sill. There were several old chairs of heavy oak, and an oak settle, nearly black with age, stood beside the wide fire-place, which was at present filled with a huge jar of 'Chinese lanterns' as all the children called Cape gooseberry. The morning sun streamed through the big stained-glass window on the landing above, and cast reflections of crim-son, blue, and yellow on the polished floor. A beautiful oak staircase ran up to it, and then turned and went on to an upper corridor. A cheerful hum of gay voices filled the place, though there was no one to be seen at the moment. As they turned to go down a passage leading to the left, Mary-Lou heard a scuttering of light feet racing along overhead, and then peals of merry laughter.

Mrs. Maynard gave her a grin. '*That* will have to stop when the first bell goes,' she said with a chuckle. 'Won't it, Len? Now, you folk, I'm leaving you here for a minute or two while I have a word with Miss Wilson. What with her going off to America at Easter on that educational tour, and our lengthy visit to the seaside, it's nearly six months since I saw her. Be good, all of you! Stephen, you stay with sisters, and don't try to wander. I know you!' And she shook her head at her son as she vanished through a door quite near, and they were left alone.

'Auntie Nell is my godmother,' said Len in a whisper. 'I'm named for her, you know – Mary Helena.'

'Is she the Head-Mistress?' asked Mary-Lou, also whis-pering.

'No – yes – well, she's one of them, anyway. The headest is Auntie Hilda– Miss Annersley. But she rang Mamma this morning before breakfast to say she had to go into Armiford early on business, so Auntie Nell would be in charge this morning.'

They lapsed into silence again, and presently the door opened and Mrs. Maynard appeared and beckoned Mary-Lou to come to her. 'Come along, Mary-Lou. I'm going to introduce you, and then I must leave you all and get back home. Goodness knows what's been happening while I've been away!' She took Mary-Lou's hand and drew her into the room. 'Here she is, Nell. This is Mary-Lou Trelawney.'

Mary-Lou looked up and found herself gazing into the face of a tall lady whose snow-white hair did not match the face itself, for that was quite young. She had clear-cut features and her eyes were dark grey, keen, but kindly. When she smiled she disclosed a row of teeth as white and perfect as Mary-Lou's own.

'So this is Mary-Lou?' she said, speaking in a very sweet mellow voice. 'I'm very glad to see you, and I hope you'll be very happy here with us. You've never been at school before, I think, so it will all be new to you.'

'No; I haven't been at school. I did lessons with Mother and Gran,' said Mary-Lou, standing very straight and square, and meeting the steady gaze with one equally steady.

Miss Wilson smiled at her again, and then turned to Mrs. Maynard. 'Are your girls here, Joey? And Stephen?' She turned back to Mary-Lou. 'Mrs. Maynard was one of my pupils when I first joined the Chalet School, and — '

'No, no, Nell!' protested that lady. 'I know what you're going to say, and it isn't fair to give me away to my own niece! No tales out of school, please!'

Miss Wilson laughed gaily. 'Very well. But if I don't, the girls certainly will! You've passed into a legend Joey.'

'*Don't* talk like that! You make me sound and feel as if I were a few hundred years old! I wasn't so bad, any-how – no worse than a good many other folk I could name.'

'No-o,' agreed Miss Wilson consideringly. 'But you did such unheard-of things, Jo. However, let's get back to Mary-Lou. I'm putting you into Upper Second, A division, Mary-Lou. Do you know Josette Russell?'

'Oh, yes,' said Mary-Lou. 'I was at the Round House the day before yesterday. And we've played together in the meadow, too.'

'That's a good thing, for I'm putting you into her form. I thought you'd have met if you knew Mrs. Maynard. We'll see how you get on there, and how you answer to school methods.'

'Is it different from learning at home?' asked Mary-Lou apprehensively.

Miss Wilson looked thoughtful. 'Yes, it is. For one thing, you will have lessons with twenty-three other girls, all more or less your own age. For another, we do some things differently – arithmetic, for instance; and geography. But I expect you will soon fall in with our ways, and then we may have to move you up. But just for this term you'll be in Upper Second A with Josette and some other very nice little folk, so I expect you'll be all right. Your mother tells me you have never learnt French, so that part will be just right for you, as it is the form where girls begin French. Although,' she added, turning to Jo Maynard, 'we've got a shock coming for the school in the way of languages. Did Hilda tell you?'

'Never a word,' returned Jo eagerly. 'What is it, Nell?'

'I'll explain in a moment. You go and bring Stephen while Mary-Lou and I have a few last words together.' Then, as Jo slipped out of the room, Miss Wilson turned to Mary-Lou, drawing her closer and holding her firmly by the shoulders. 'I want to say this to you, Mary-Lou. You may find a good many difficult things coming along, as you're not used to school ways. Don't be afraid. They won't be difficulties long. Stand up to them if you can; but if they are too much for you, then ask to see either Miss Annersley or me, and we'll talk them over and try to find a way out. Do you understand, child?'

'Yes, thank you,' said Mary-Lou with one of her queerly blue-eyed looks. 'But – but I *like* things that are difficult.'

Miss Wilson broke into her clear, ringing laugh again. 'Oh, you'll do!' she exclaimed. 'You were just born to be a school-girl! Now run along and see what adventures you can find!' And she gave the little girl a gentle push towards the door.

Mary-Lou gave her a beaming smile. Then, with a sudden memory of all she had heard from the Maynards and the Russells, she picked up the skirt of her tunic, bent her knees in a little bob-curtsey, and finally found herself on the other side of the door, just as Stephen marched in with a cry of 'Hello, Auntie Nell! I'm here!'

Sybil Russell was standing with the Triplets and their mother, and she said quickly, 'Hello, Mary-Lou! Come along and I'll show you where to go. 'Bye, Auntie! See you on Saturday, and thanks awfully.' Then she laid a hand on Mary-Lou's shoulder and steered her off, barely giving her time to say good-bye to her aunt.

'Which form?' she asked as they reached the hall.

'Upper Second A. Same as Josette,' replied Mary-Lou.

'Good! She'll give you a hand if you need it. Josette's young for it – she isn't nine till December – but she's clever. Got half my brains as well as her own share. Ailie may be brainy, too, but you can't really tell at just four.'

'Aren't you clever, then?'

'Not in the least,' returned Sybil cheerfully. 'Oh, I try – in spots, anyway; but I'm not much use. I like sewing and art much better than lessons.'

'*Sewing!*' gasped Mary-Lou with a vivid memory of many battles with Gran over sewing. 'You don't really *like* sewing, do you?'

'Rather! Mummy has promised me that if I work hard at all my other lessons and get through School Cert. I can go to the Art Needlework School at South Kensington for two years when I'm seventeen. That's what I want to do, you know. Embroidery of every kind, and make my own designs. It'll be heavenly! But I've got to get my School Cert. first, so it means slogging at lessons, whether I like them or not. Now, here we are. Josette won't be here just yet, because we've only just come, and we haven't reported in the library yet. But I'll find someone to look after you till she comes. You'll be all right then.'

So saying, she pushed open a door and went in, Mary-Lou following closely at her heels. That young woman

45

found herself in a big sunny room, where about a dozen little girls of her own age or a little older were all gabbling away as hard as they could. Only one sat demurely at a desk, her hands folded on its lid, her eyes gazing out into the garden.

The gabbling ceased on the entrance of the pair, and everyone turned to look. Two or three small people detached themselves from the main group and came racing to meet them. Foremost of them was a very pretty little person with a mop of golden-brown curls tied back from a round little face whose principal feature was a pair of dark but vividly purple-blue eyes, like purple pansies.

'Vi Lucy! Just the one I want!' said Sybil. 'Julie's here, I suppose? And Betsy? How's Aunt Janie and the new baby?'

'Splendid, both of them. The baby's to be christened on Sunday, and we three are all going home for it. She's to be called Katharine Margaret. Is this a new girl for us?'

'Yes. Her name is Mary-Lou Trelawney, and she lives next door to Auntie Jo. Find her a desk, Vi, and see she knows what to do and where to go. I s'pose Betsy's in our form-room?'

'I 'spect so. She said she was going early 'cos she wanted to bag decent desks for her and you. Did you say her name's Mary-Lou, Sybil? How awfully funny!'

'I don't see it,' retorted Sybil, turning on her heel. 'You stay with Vi Lucy, Mary-Lou. She'll see to you till Josette comes along.' And she departed.

Left alone with twelve complete strangers, Mary-Lou tilted her chin and gave them look for look. It was something of an ordeal, but she wasn't going to be stared down by any other girl – not if she knew it!

Vi, who was one of the friendliest little souls in the world, smiled at her. 'I didn't mean to be rude about your name, Mary-Lou; but it *is* funny, just the same. You'll understand when you know. You see, we've got another new girl with a double name – Verity-Ann. That's her!' And she pointed unashamedly at the girl who was still sitting at her desk. 'Lot's of us *have* more than one name, of course – I'm Mary Viola myself – but we don't use the other. So it *is* funny to have two new girls at once who both do. Now, isn't it?'

'I s'pose it is,' conceded Mary-Lou. 'What are the rest called?'

'Oh, this is Hilda Davies; and those others are Eileen Johnson, Margaret Jones, Lesley Malcolm, Doris Hill, Iris Wells and Mary Leigh. And those two over there are Anne and Angela Carter. They're twins, but you'd never think it to look at them, would you?'

'I'm Gwen Davis,' added an eleven-year-old with a mop of brown curls and a freckled face. 'I say! You really aren't Mary-Lou, are you? I mean, that wasn't what you were christened?'

'Well, it's Mary Louise, really,' admitted Mary-Lou, 'after Gran and Grannie – but Grannie's dead. But you couldn't say that all the time.' She lowered her voice: 'Is *she* truthfully Verity-Ann?' She nodded in the direction of the solitary little girl at the desk who was still gazing out of the window and taking no apparent notice of the rest of them.

'Well, she says so. Come on and speak to her,' said Vi. 'You two ought to be chums, both having double names.'

The eleven pulled her over to the desk, and Vi introduced the pair. 'This is Mary-Lou Trelawney, Verity-Ann, and she's a new girl too. She can have this next desk to you 'cos it almost makes you twins, doesn't it, both using two names? You have this desk, Mary-Lou, and – Why, Phil Craven! I thought you said you weren't coming back 'cos your people were going to South Africa!' For the door had opened once more, and a little girl with hair screwed tightly off a thin sallow face entered with a sulky look. 'Why didn't you come yesterday like the rest of us?'

The form, led by Vi, promptly thronged round the newcomer with shouts and exclamations, and the two new girls were left alone.

47

CHAPTER FIVE

NEW EXPERIENCES

MARY-LOU felt rather shy as she sat down at the desk Vi Lucy had pointed out, and turned to look at the other new girl.

'I'm bigger than she is,' she thought a little triumphantly, and truthfully, for Mary-Lou was a well-grown young person and Verity-Ann was altogether on a miniature scale. 'She's jolly pretty, but she's tiny, too – a bit like a big doll. Wonder what she's like inside?'

At this point, Verity-Ann turned her head and gave Mary-Lou a cool stare which rather disconcerted that young woman. It was so oddly critical. However, she was a friendly enough little girl, so she leaned over and half-whispered, 'I'm as new as you. Do you think you are going to like it?'

Verity-Ann looked at her again. 'I doubt it,' she said, speaking in her tiny, silvery voice, which just matched her appearance.

'But why?' demanded Mary-Lou. 'It's *my* first school too, 'cos I've always done lessons with Mother and Gran up to this. But I quite think I'll like it when I'm 'customed to it. What did you do?'

'I had a governess,' returned Verity-Ann, sighing in an elderly way. 'My mother is dead, and my father is away. I lived with my grandparents in Yorkshire. Now both of them are dead.'

'I see. And so you've been sent to school like me? Did you say your father was away? So's mine.'

'My father is abroad,' Verity-Ann said in a superior way.

'So's mine. He's up the Amazon in South America somewhere.'

Verity-Ann's small face grew faintly pink. 'That is where my father is. He is with the Mur-ray-Cameron Ex-pe-di-tion,' she said the long word with care, 'where they are exploring some of the con-confluents. He has been away for quite a long time, and I really cannot be said to know him at all.'

Mary-Lou stared at this stilted way of putting it – as well she might! Until she had met Clem and Tony her own English had been fairly correct, but never had she heard even a grown-up speak like this. However, she persevered with the job of making friends with this queer girl, though she privately thought it uphill work.

'I expect it's the same as my father is with,' she said.

'It seems probable,' assented Verity-Ann. Then she relaxed a little to ask, 'What is he doing?'

'In the Amazon, d'you mean? He collects butterflies and insects and things,' his daughter replied vaguely. 'What's your father do?'

'He is a – a cart-og-grapher. That means that he makes maps,' Verity-Ann kindly explained, as Mary-Lou stared at her blankly. 'He is quite famous for his maps.'

'So's my dad for his c'llections!' Mary-Lou wasn't going to be outdone. 'Some of them are in the British Museum, and he's written a book about the butterflies of – somewhere in Asia. He hasn't seen me for seven years, when I was just a small kid. I'll be a surprise to him when we *do* meet, shan't I?' And she gave a delighted giggle.

What neither of the little girls knew was that there was grave anxiety about the Murray-Cameron Expedition, since nothing had been heard of it for more than ten months. The last news had taken a long time to get through, so that it was now eighteen months old, and there was reason to fear that calamity had overtaken the venture in some form.

Verity-Ann screwed up her face. 'Do you really use

49

slang?' she asked in tones that would have been suitable if she had asked if Mary-Lou used poison.

Mary-Lou stared. 'What've I said that's slang?' she demanded. 'Are you a goody-good?'

Resentment flamed in Verity-Ann's eyes, but before she could reply the door opened again, and a very pretty young lady walked in, followed by a string of small girls.

A shout went up at the sight. 'Oh, Miss Linton! Are you going to be our form-mistress this year?'

Miss Linton laughed. 'Good morning, everyone! Yes, I am indeed. And I hope you people are all prepared to be very good and work very hard.'

'We can *try*, I s'pose,' Vi said doubtfully.

'I hope you will! Well, now run to your seats, those of you who have them. Then we can see where we are. Any new girls not already seated, stand over there till we find places for you.'

Three girls stood to the side, while the rest scuttled to their seats, among them Josette Russell, who flashed a chummy grin at Mary-Lou before she sat down. Miss Linton nodded as she looked over the room and then turned to ask the names of the shy trio against the wall. They proved to be Rosamund Williams, Celia James, and Ruth Barnes. She sent them to various unoccupied desks, and then glanced round again, singling out Mary-Lou and Verity-Ann at once.

'You are the two people with double names, I expect,' she said with her charming smile. 'Miss Annersley said I should have you. Which is which of you?'

'I'm Mary-Lou Trelawney,' Mary-Lou responded cheerfully. 'This is Verity-Ann – what's your other name?' she added doubtfully to Verity-Ann.

'My name is Verity-Ann Carey,' the name's owner replied with dignity.

'Thank you,' said Miss Linton. 'Well, I can't have you sitting together, I think. Lesley Malcolm, suppose you change with Mary-Lou. *That's* better!' as Lesley got up with a grimace at her next-door neighbour which the mistress did not see. 'Now, where's my register?'

Looking towards the door from her seat by Josette, Mary-Lou saw that a very dignified person with chestnut hair worn in a large knob at the back of her neck had come in, bearing a sheaf of thin, paper-covered books, one of which she handed to Miss Linton, saying quietly, 'Miss Dene asked me to say that she's sorry the registers are so late, Miss Linton, but there was so much to do, she finished them only this morning. Miss Wilson says that Prayers will be at nine-thirty to give everyone time to get properly settled.'

'Thank you, Gillian.' Miss Linton glanced at her watch. 'Just twenty-five minutes, then. That gives me nice time to take register and announce the names of the form officials.'

'Yes, thank you.' Gillian smiled at the mistress and went off, and Miss Linton opened the book, took up her fountain pen and said, 'Quiet, children. I'm going to take register.'

Instant silence prevailed as she attended to that duty. Then she closed the book, handed it to Vi, and asked her to take it to the secretary and tell her that everyone was present. Vi ran away, looking important, and Miss Linton smiled at the expectant crowd. 'When Vi comes back I'll give out the names of the form officials,' she said, taking up a slip of paper she had laid down on the desk when she came in.

Mary-Lou gave a little wriggle of excitement. Whatever were 'Form officials?' It sounded most awfully grand!

It sounded grander still when Vi had returned and she heard that the Form President was Vi herself; Josette Russell was Flower Lady; Mistress of the Inkwells was Gwen Davies; the Porter was Doris Hill; Lady Tidiness was Angela Carter; and Lesley Malcolm was Form Messenger.

'High Duster of the Blackboard – Josefa Wertheim,' read out Miss Linton. 'Chief Opener of Windows –

Gretchen Mensch.' She nodded at a dark, foreign-looking child as she spoke, and the grave little face broke into a smile.

Mary-Lou looked at her with interest. What a funny name she had – Josefa too! Not a bit like English names! But 'Auntie Jo' had told her that there were some foreign girls at the Chalet School, and they were expecting more this term.

'Younger sisters and children of old girls who haven't been able to send their children to us before,' she had said airily. 'Of course, when the school was in Tirol we had more of those than English. It's the other way on now, though I expect when we return we shall change round again.'

Gretchen must be one of these foreigners, and Josefa another. How pretty *she* was with her golden curls and violet-blue eyes! Just like a fairy-tale princess, thought Mary-Lou, little knowing that Josefa's mother had been known as 'Cinders' in her own Chalet School days for that same fairy-tale beauty, and that *her* elder sister was always remembered as the loveliest girl the school had ever known. Later on, when the small girl met Maria von Glück, Wanda's eldest girl, who was a shining light of Three A, she could well believe it.

But Miss Linton was still speaking, so Mary-Lou listened.

'You must all appoint your own deputy in case any of you should be absent,' she was saying, 'though I hope you won't be. New girls, remember are eligible for deputies. Now there goes the bell for Prayers, so we must finish up after. Form, in two lines! Old girls look after the new ones. Josefa, lead your line to the Gym; the rest follow Vi. Forward – *quietly*, please!'

Mary-Lou had noticed that while they were lining up at the door the mistress had spoken once or twice, moving various people to one half of the line or the other. She wondered what it meant, but said nothing. Later on she discovered that a number of the girls were Catholics, and had their prayers with Miss Wilson, also a Catholic, in the Gym, while the bulk of the school went to Hall, where Miss Annersley usually presided. As she was absent this morning, her place was taken by a tall, very broad lady whom she later knew as Mrs. Redmond, a former mistress, who had lost both husband and little daughter, and had been glad to come back to the school and find work to fill her empty life. She was senior mistress, and responsible for a good deal of the Senior English. She conducted the little service in a pleasant voice. They sang a hymn; then there was the reading of the Parable of the Talents by the head-girl; then they had two or three collects, Our Father, and a blessing. When it was over and they had all risen from their knees, a door at the bottom of the great room opened, and the rest of the school came in. The mistresses followed them, and Miss Wilson went up to the dais, where Mrs. Redmond stood down from the reading-desk to make room for her.

'Sit down, everyone,' said Miss Wilson. Then, when they were all sitting quietly on the long forms that ran across the room in three aisles, she went on quietly, 'I haven't much to say to you just now, for Miss Annersley will give you her usual talk to-morrow. But I want to welcome you all, and wish you a very happy term. The exam successes are posted up on the notice-boards, so you can read them at your leisure. But I feel sure that those of you who knew her will be pleased to hear that Daisy Venables, who left us two years ago to study medicine at London, has won the Ransome Gold Medal with a paper on infectious diseases of children. It is a new award, and Daisy is the first to win it, so we may all be very proud of her. Several more old girls obtained various degrees last term. There isn't time to go through the list now, but their names are up on the Honours Boards.'

She made a little pause to allow for the clapping, during which Mary-Lou sat round-eyed, firmly clutching the tiny hand Verity-Ann had slipped into hers. School, it seemed was going to prove much more exciting than she had thought. If only Clem were here too! But Clem was some-where in the Outer Hebrides, and far away.

'Now, I have an announcement to make,' the mistress said, and her keen grey eyes were twinkling. 'As most of you know, the Chalet School was begun in Tirol, where the people speak a form of German, and only left there when things became impossible. But those of us who were part of the school in those days have always hoped that the time would come when we should be able to return. It can't be yet, of course; but it seems to be coming in sight at last. In those days, as we had girls of many European nations, as well as British and American, we were tri-lingual – that is, little ones, we all learned to speak in three languages – English, French, and German. We had girls from Denmark, Holland, Norway, France, Italy, Russia, and a good many other places, but we didn't ask anyone to learn more than the three – though Joe Bettany, now known to most of you as Mrs. Maynard, certainly did her best to learn the lot!'

A chuckle went round the Sixth at this; but they were all deeply interested in Miss Wilson's speech, so no one said anything. She joined in the chuckle before she went on: 'Since we have been in England, there has been so much to do that conversational German has been dropped altogether except for those girls who needed it for examina-tions; and French has been cut down to only one day a week. The Juniors were not even asked for that much. But now we must begin again, and brush up our languages in good earnest. Therefore,' she leaned forward on the reading-desk and spoke very impressively, 'we are going back to the old ways. English, French, and German will be spoken on alternate days, so that each has a turn twice a week, with the chance of speaking just what you like on Sundays. Also, after eleven o'clock on Saturdays you will also speak which you like. As most of you are British, English will always be a Saturday language.'

The school at large was too well trained to groan, but what they thought was plain to read in their faces. Miss

Wilson smiled at the horror she saw there before she continued briskly, 'Now, none of us wish to make life too hard for you, so at first things will be easy. For the first fortnight of the term you will be helped where you need it, so long as you really do try to keep the rule. After that, any Senior breaking it will be fined a halfpenny for each mistake; Middles, a farthing; and Juniors, until half-term a halfpenny for every *ten* mistakes. The fines will go to our free beds in the Sanatorium. But as we propose to hold our annual Sale of Work next term for that purpose, we don't want the fines to grow too much. So be careful, girls! Almost all the mistresses can speak both French and German fluently, and they will help you when you need it. Later, I hope that will not be necessary. To the Juniors I want to say, ask someone who knows to put what you wish to say into the language for the day, and try to repeat it properly. If you do that, you will soon learn.'

The Juniors looked doubtful, but no one dared voice her thoughts. But Miss Wilson had certainly thrown a bombshell into their midst. She said no more, but called for 'the King,' and when it had been sung, they marched out to their form-rooms, beginning with the tinies, and ending with the Sixth, and presently Mary-Lou found herself once again in the sunny form-room with a lively protest going on all around her.

'It's all very well for you people,' cried Lesley Malcolm to Josefa and Gretchen. 'You speak German at home, I know. But what about *us*? I can't think how we're going to manage at all!'

'We may speak German, but we don't speak French,' retorted Josefa. 'We shall be just as bad at that as anyone – except the French people. I don't know a word of it.'

'I don't know a word of either!' wailed Doris Hill. 'I shan't have a penny all the term – I *know* I shan't!'

'Don't be silly, Doris,' said Miss Linton, who had come in just in time to hear this. 'Most of you folk don't know a word of either, and you're no worse off than anyone else. Now listen to me, all of you. When it's a French or German day, you must think what you want to say, and then ask any of us mistresses to put it into the language for you, and practise saying it over and over again till you can say it properly. We mistresses will say what we have to say very slowly at first until you grasp what we are saying, and that way you'll soon find you know a number of words and phrases. At the very worst we will turn it into English. But of course we shall say it in which ever language it *should* be again. If you all try hard, you'll find by half-term that you can speak a little; and by the end of term you will know quite a good deal. Believe me, I *know*! I've been through it in my time, you see.'

And just then a small voice was uplifted. 'Please, I don't think I approve at all of speaking German,' it said distinctly.

There was a sensation. Everyone turned to look at the speaker -- Verity-Ann. She sat there, her cheeks very pink, but her small pointed jaw set obstinately.

'You'd better discuss that with Miss Annersley or Miss Wilson,' said Miss Linton, when she had recovered her breath.

'Thank you. I think perhaps it *would* be better,' said Verity-Ann soberly.

Most of the girls looked 'What cheek!' at each other. Miss Linton, however, knew it for what it was. Six years of practice had taught her how to distinguish between cheek and simplicity. Inwardly, she was greatly amused, and she wondered what the two Heads would make of this startlingly self-possessed mite. However, that was no business of hers, so she went on with the day's work.

'Phil Craven, will you be Stationery? 'she asked. 'Anne Carter, I want you to be responsible for text-books. Phil, I hope you'll be careful. It's an important post, you know.'

Phil said, 'Yes, Miss Linton,' very sulkily; but Anne beamed with satisfaction, and so did her twin.

The next thing was to see to text-books. Miss Linton told the old girls to take everything out of their desks, and then went the rounds, confiscating here, returning there, till at last all literature and sundry other books stood

56

in neat piles on the floor, and the girls returned a much depleted store to their desks.

The next thing was to get the new books, and, greatly to her joy, Mary-Lou was sent off with Anne to the stock-room to help to bring them back. A sunny-faced senior, Gay Lambert, met them at the door and directed them to a table presided over by one Jacynth Hardy. Later the small girl was to hear something of Jacynth's story, and that she and Gay were close friends. At present, she looked rather awe-strickenly at the slight, grey-eyed Senior. The sad face broke into a smile on hearing her name as Anne said, 'Please, Jacynth, can Mary-Lou and me have our lit'rature books?'

'*Really*, Mary-Lou?' she asked, as she turned to pick up a little pile of *Hereward the Wake* and put them into Anne's arms.

'Yes,' said Mary-Lou for herself.

Anne gave a delighted giggle. 'She's not the *only* one,' she said meaningly.

Jacynth stared at her, but before she could ask any further questions, one of the mistresses came in to demand her text-books for Form Two B, the Senior quickly piled the required literature books in the arms of the small pair, and then turned to attend to Miss Edwards' wants.

Back in the form-room, Miss Linton soon had the literature distributed, and then called up Mary-Lou again to go and bring other books, while Anne was sent over to the Annexe for ink, chalk, and other necessities. 'Take Verity-Ann and Ruth Barnes with you, and ask Jacynth to give you everything else,' the young mistress said. 'I know what it's like in the stock-room at the beginning of the year, and they'll be thankful to be rid of one form, anyhow.'

Verity-Ann rose in her composed little way, and Ruth, a jolly-looking youngster of eleven, as new as the other two, came likewise.

'Come on,' said Mary-Lou once they were outside. 'This way!'

'What's Jacynth like?' asked Ruth. 'She's got a pretty name. It'll do for my c'llection. I'm c'llecting pretty names,' she added in explanation.

' 'Sh!' said Mary-Lou. 'We mustn't talk here. Do buck up, Verity-Ann!' And she sped ahead, followed by Ruth with Verity-Ann following at a more sedate pace.

In the stock-room they found girls from almost every form collecting books, and it was two or three minutes before Jacynth was able to attend to them. At last she was free, and turned with a friendly smile to Mary-Lou as she held out her hand for the list Miss Linton had given them.

'There's one thing,' she said as she scanned it, 'no one can forget who *you* are with a double-barrel name like that!'

'Oh, I'm not the only one,' returned Mary-Lou airily. 'This is Verity-Ann Carey.'

Jacynth gasped. 'Mary-Lou – Verity-Ann!' she exclaimed. 'Well I'm blest!' She turned to Ruth. 'And what's *your* name? Don't say you're Sophia-Jane to complete the trio!'

Ruth flushed up. 'I'm Ruth Barnes,' she said, rather offendedly. 'I haven't *got* a second name.'

'Let's be thankful for so much! Now to business. Yes; these are all ready for you. Here you are.' And she took a pile from a near-by shelf. 'Arithmetic, history, geography, *La Vie de Madame Souris*, atlas. I think — No! Here, you – Ruth. You want *The Parables and Miracles of Jesus*. Here you are! Now, can you carry all those without falling over anything or dropping half of them?'

'Yes, thank you,' said Verity-Ann, speaking in her tiny, silvery voice, which was, nevertheless, so clear.

'Then off you go! Goodness knows there are enough folk milling around here without you folk!'

They departed, to find when they reached their form-room that someone had put piles of new exercise-books on their desks, as well as pens, pencils, blotting-paper, and various other oddments. They were given lockers in which

58

to keep their books, with a word of warning from Miss Linton as to the need for neatness, and the penalty attached to untidness. By the time they had packed everything in, the bell was ringing for the mid-morning Break, and they all marched to what was known as the Buttery for milk and cocoa and three biscuits each. When they had finished this, they were 'shooed' off outside by a vigilant prefect, and told to play till the bell rang again.

As soon as Gay Lambert had left, most of them crowded round Verity-Ann, all agog to find out *why* she didn't want to learn German.

'The Germans are a most unpleasant people,' she told them primly. 'I don't wish to have anything to do with any language of theirs.'

'Well, you've a good cheek to talk as you did to Miss Linton!' cried Vi Lucy. 'You can't speak to a mistress that way! You'll get into rows *and* rows if you try it on!'

'What will you say to the Heads?' asked Lesley curiously.

'I shall tell them just the same thing,' was the stately answer.

'Won't they stare!' This was Gretchen Mensch. 'Anyhow, if you want to come with us when we go back to Tirol, you'll just *have* to be able to speak it– or be dumb!'

'I doubt if my guardian would wish me to go so far,' replied Verity-Ann stiffly. 'I think it most unlikely.'

'Oh, she's dippy!' Vi cried disgustedly. 'Don't let's waste time on her! Come on, you people; let's play Tag! I'll be He!'

They scattered to their game at once, and presently only Mary-Lou and Verity-Ann were left under the big chestnut tree beneath which they had been gathered. They stared at each other. Mary-Lou was the first to break silence.

'Don't you think it would be – *wizard* to go to Tirol?' she asked.

'If you mean it would be very pleasant – no, I don't,' said Verity-Ann decidedly.

'Well, I should like to see other countries – like Father,

you know. Tirol 'ud be a beginning. I don't s'pose it's very far really.'

Verity-Ann tossed her golden curls. 'You had better go and play with the others. I must think all this over.'

What Mary-Lou might have done, it is hard to say. She was half-offended at being treated like this by someone of her own age; but she was also rather intrigued by the very 'difference' of Verity-Ann. However, before she could make up her mind what to say or do, a long string of small girls, clinging hand to hand, swooped down on them and gathered them in. Josette Russell grabbed Mary-Lou by a pigtail with a gasping 'Caught!' but Verity-Ann shook herself free with much dignity.

'I do not wish to play, thank you,' she said, her small nose in the air.

They let her go in sheer amazement and she turned her back on them and stalked off to the side of the great lawn, while Josette, dropping her neighbour's hand, exclaimed breathlessly, 'In here, Mary-Lou! Come on! There's Lesley over there!' And the whole string tore off after the agile Lesley, racing at top speed, and screaming like a dozen or more hysterical steam-engines.

When Break finally came to an end, they were glowing, breathless, and untidy, and it took them all their time to tear to the Splasheries to make themselves fit to be seen and then scuttle off to their form-room before the second bell rang. Verity-Ann was sitting at her desk when they poured pell-mell into the room, looking almost provokingly neat and clean.

Miss Linton came a minute or two later to settle them and dictate their time-table to them. Then she gave them their homework, and the bell for the end of morning school rang as they wrote the last sum down.

On Tuesdays and Thursdays, Mary-Lou was to go home for lunch. Other days she must stay till half-past three for games, art, and needle-work. And on Saturday mornings there would be Brownie meeting. To-day, she packed her new books together with a bunch of 'name-labels' into her new satchel; tucked a fairy-story Vi Lucy had lent her under one arm, and took a pencil-box in the other hand. Then she departed, to be met by Mother at the bottom of the avenue.

'Well, dear?' said Mother rather anxiously. 'How have you got on?'

'All right, thank you,' Mary-Lou replied thoughtfully. 'It might be worse.'

'What *do* you mean?' Mother asked as they got into the bus.

'Well, it *might* be worse. There are some quite decent people there,' Mary-Lou returned.

'Then you think you will like it?'

'Oh, yes; I think I shall like it all right,' her small daughter told her. Inwardly, Mary-Lou was decided that Clem had been right after all, and school was really very jolly.

CHAPTER SIX

AN ENIGMA

By the end of three weeks, Mary-Lou had found her feet and had settled down as a complete schoolgirl. She was one of a little crowd of friends led by Josette Russell and Vi Lucy; 'loathed' Miss Edwards, who was unlucky enough to be responsible for their arithmetic; 'adored' Miss Linton, who took all English subjects; started half a dozen hobbies, picked up slang, had wild enthusiasms, and grumbled as all the rest did.

In form she did well in Miss Linton's subjects, for she liked them, and what Mary-Lou liked, she did well. In arithmetic she dropped nearly to bottom, however, for she was not mathematically inclined, and had hitherto learned from Gran, whose methods were those of her own schooldays. What she knew, she knew thoroughly – Gran had seen to that! In tables and 'mental' she was well above the average. But when it came to 'sums' she found that she had to unlearn a good deal of what she had already learnt, and this made things harder for her. Moreover, Miss Edwards expected them to work to time, and if she said a sum had to be finished in ten minutes, finished it had to be, or you lost marks. Mary-Lou, accustomed to going at her own pace, found this a real handicap, and her marks were often shamefully low.

Geography began by being another snag, since she had been taught as small girls were taught in the late 'eighties of the last century; but Miss Wilson knew how to make her lessons interesting, and Mary-Lou, once she had got accustomed to the new methods, found that she was learning fast, and 'jography' was well on the way to becoming one of her favourite subjects. As for French, she soon proved that she had a real gift for languages, and forged ahead at a speed that made the rest of the form declare that she must be having coaching at home.

'I'm not – oh, I'm not!' Mary-Lou protested vigorously. 'Gran says she's forgotten most of the French she ever knew, and I haven't been near Mother for a week 'cos she's got another cold, and Gran said she wasn't going to have *me* sneezing and sniffling all over the place! So now!'

"Well, we all began together,' grumbled Lesley Malcolm, 'and look what miles you are ahead of us!'

'P'r'aps she's got French somewhere in her family and she inherits it,' suggested Vi, who had overheard her mother say that Julie, the eldest in their family, had inherited her love of reading from their father.

'Go on!' Josette said sceptically. 'I don't believe you can inherit French – not grammar, anyhow!'

'Well, it's queer; that's all;' And there they had to leave it.

Verity-Ann, on the other hand, was no nearer being one of them than she had been the very first day.

Listen in to a conversation in the staff-room when the term was about a month old.

'The little Mary-Lou does well,' Mlle Berné declared one evening, looking up from some exercises. 'If she continues, she should be ready for Lower Third by the end of this term.'

'Not in arithmetic,' said Miss Edwards firmly. 'She's so much to unlearn that it's going to take me all that time to get her into modern methods. And she's not brilliant at it at the best of times.'

'What do you folk make of that other small thing with the double name?' demanded Miss Linton, putting her elbows on the table and cupping her chin in her hands.

'Verity-Ann Carey? I don't know what she's like for most of you, but she and Mary-Lou and young Lesley and Doris Hill will drive me into the nearest asylum unless something happens!' retorted Miss Edwards.

'She does very poor work for me,' Mademoiselle sighed. 'I may be mistaken, but it seems to me that she *despises* my language and will not try. She is *terrible*!'

'She could be excellent at composition if she would only stop using the stilted language of fifty or sixty years ago,' Miss Linton said with a chuckle. 'Believe it or not, she calls flowers "floral gems". And she never condescends to speak of "the sky" – oh dear, no! It's "the heavens!" And her history is the limit, mostly strings of dates. She reads aloud delightfully; but her writing! The most *awful* Italian hand, and so difficult to read!'

'Don't that crowd get transcription?' asked Miss Slater, the senior maths mistress.

'Of course they do – three times a week, thirty minutes each time. But do you think my lady will change her style to any form of script? Not she! She listens to all I have to say, and then goes on copying whatever they *are* copying in her own wicked way.'

'You'd better put Davidson on to her,' suggested Miss Wilson, who happened to be with them. 'Hi, Nest! Wake up there! Open your ears, my girl, and listen to our troubles.'

Miss Davidson, the junior art mistress, looked up with a start from the novel in which she had been buried fathoms deep, to ask, 'What is it? I wasn't listening.'

'That was quite obvious. Listen now! Do you teach your young hopefuls in the Second lettering by any chance?'

'*Lettering*? To kids of that age? Is it likely?'

'I don't see why not. Not that Black Letter stuff, of course; but what about script at its most beautiful, with borders round. That would be good for their design, too. Couldn't they do that?'

'I hadn't thought of it,' said Miss Davidson, staring. 'Why on earth are you, of all people, fussing about their art?'

'Don't say "you, of all people" as if I had no art in my soul! I'm as keen on it as the average person —'

'In fact, you don't pretend to know much about it, but you do know what you like,' suggested Miss Davidson solemnly.

'Oh, it's a little better than that. But what we really want is your help for Gillian. She has an obstinate youngster who flatly refuses to use any kind of script, but writes in a most appalling version of old-fashioned Italian hand.

'Which of the imps is that?' asked Miss Davidson with sudden interest. When she heard Verity-Ann's name, she groaned loudly. 'Oh, my dears! *That* child! She's the most awful of the lot! Not an ounce of imagination in her. Set them to do an illustration, and she produces a thing that a K.G. baby would be ashamed of!'

'Dear me!' Miss Wilson said mildly. 'We seem to have gathered a poor thing into the fold this time. Can't anyone say *anything* for her?'

No one could, it seemed, and there was a pause. Then Gillian Linton leaned back in her chair. 'I think,' she said slowly, 'that it's not so much "can't" as "won't".' She turned to Miss Wilson, who had taught her when she herself had been a pupil at the school. 'Bill, think it over. Don't you agree?'

'But *why*?' Miss Slater demanded with round-eyed astonishment.

'Well, I may be wrong, but I have a feeling that she may do it from a sense of loyalty to whoever taught her before. Bill, you ought to know. What are her roots?'

'A motherless child with an explorer father who has been somewhere up the Amazon for the last seven years. She was brought up by very elderly grandparents and a governess who was a friend of the old lady's and somewhere in the seventies herself, I believe. They didn't approve of school for small girls, and there was no one else suitable. By the way, Commander Carey is with the same expedition as Professor Trelawney, and – or so old Mrs. Trelawney told me when she came to see us about Mary-Lou – there is a good deal of anxiety about it. They haven't been heard from for some time – nearly two years, I believe.'

The Staff looked serious at this.

'Do you think the children know?' Mlle Berné asked.

Miss Wilson shook her head. 'Mary-Lou certainly has no idea. About Verity-Ann I shouldn't like to say. The arrangements here were made for her by her grandfather's lawyer, who is her trustee, and I don't know what she may have been told. But if Verity-Ann is being silly and obstinate about her work with the idea of remaining loyal to an old governess, someone will have to talk seriously to the child when there's a chance.'

The subject dropped after that, and the Staff turned to other things. But the mistresses were by no means the only people to be puzzled by Verity-Ann. As those grandees were discussing the school problems, the prefects – or some of them – were doing the same thing at a select party held in the head-girl's study.

The room was a small one, but six people managed to cram themselves into it somehow. The head-girl herself sat

C

in the one armchair it boasted, and on one arm sat the first of her great allies, Gay Lambert of the yellow curls, sunny blue eyes, and impish smile, and on the other the third of the Triumvirate as they were known among the compeers – Jacynth Hardy, as unlike Gay with her serious grey eyes and smooth black hair brushed severely from her broad brows as she could be. Mollie Avery had perched herself on the table, which was in imminent danger of collapse, as it was rickety, to put it kindly, and Mollie no lightweight. Brown-eyed Nancy Canton squatted on the floor hugging her knees up to her chin; and Janet Scott, a quiet, clever-looking girl from Edinburgh, occupied the only other chair in the room.

'I rather like that new kid – what's her name – Mary-Lou,' said Gay idly in a pause in their conversation. 'She's a sporting little bloke— '

'Your language!' ejaculated Mollie.

'Your fussiness!' Gay retorted.

'Dry up, you two!' Gillian put in at this point with some firmness. 'What put the kid into your head all of a sudden, Gay?'

'I was just thinking of the netball prac I took with her lot this afternoon. She's picked up the game jolly well, and should make a very decent goal defence when she's steadied a little. She's all over the shop just now, of course – *ubique*, in fact, eh, Jean?' And Gay grinned at Janet, who gave a sudden chuckle.

'You're right,' Nancy agreed from her lowly position. 'But what about that other infant – Verity-Ann, isn't she called? D'you think she's crackers by any chance?'

'*Crackers*? What on earth do you mean?' demanded Gillian.

'I think she's normal enough,' put in Jacynth thoughtfully. 'She's rather quieter than that crowd, and her manners, not to speak of her language, remind one of the people in that ghastly *Mother's Influence*. How would it be to turn Gay on to her. They might reform each other.

66

Gay could teach Verity-Ann to be more – more colloquial, and Verity-Ann could make Gay more — '

'Yes? More what?' interrupted Gay, a gleam in her eyes.

'More ladylike in conversation,' returned Jacynth sweetly.

'Shut up, you two!' Gillian grabbed Gay and held her down firmly. 'There isn't room to rag here. If you go on with it, I'll turf you out. So beware!'

Gay subsided, and Nancy went on placidly with what she had been saying. 'I'm not objecting to her manners. I rather think most of that crew could do with a touch or two of the elegancies. But look here, Gill! Last evening after supper I went to the Gym to get my blazer. The entire boiling were there, playing games – Touch Last and Twos-and-Three and things like that. They were yelling their heads off, of course, and having a jolly good time – all but this queer infant. She, if you please, was sitting in a corner by herself, *doing embroidery*! I ask you – at *that* age! I got hold of Vi Lucy and Jo Russell and asked them what they meant by leaving her out of their fun – Mary-Lou, I may say, was up to her eyes in it, yelling away with the best! They both fired up – quite mad, they sounded – and said they *had* asked her; they always did. But she said she didn't approve of such hoydenish games. Oh, they were wild enough, those two! And where, may I ask, did a scrap like that pick up such a word as "hoydenish"? I'll bet none of *them* had ever heard it before.'

'She didn't *approve*?' demanded Jacynth, sitting up so suddenly on her arm that she nearly overbalanced and fell headlong into the grate. 'But – Great stars and garters! How old is this infant?'

'Oh, ten or eleven, I suppose. She may be nine – or twelve, though she doesn't look anything like that. Haven't they one or two nine-year-old prodigies in that form, Gill?'

'How on earth should I know? Why do you ask, Gay?'

'I just wondered. I haven't had much to do with that

67

crowd this term. What with one thing and another, I'm pretty full up, and any spare time I've got goes to my 'cello. But didn't I hear Joanna had some sort of a barney with her last week?'

'You did – over talking German. Anyone know the exact story?' And Nancy glanced round inquiringly.

'So far as I could understand, Joanna was awfully riled about it, though she only told me unofficially. Verity-Ann told her that she didn't approve of the Germans *or* their language, and she doesn't talk at all on German days rather than use it.'

Gay began to laugh. 'What a nerve! Does she say that sort of thing to the Staff, d'you think? There'll be fireworks with some of them if she does – Matey, for instance.'

'I've no idea. I should imagine so far as *they* are concerned, she keeps her opinions to herself. Can you imagine yourself telling Miss Edwards or even Miss Linton that you wouldn't talk if you mightn't use your own language, and disapproved of what the school insists on?' demanded Gillian with more force than good grammar. 'I most certainly can *not*! I should expect to be swallowed whole if I did. Miss Linton is a pet, but I'm sure she wouldn't stand for that, let alone Miss Edwards, who can be as sarkey as Bill when she gets going.'

'I wonder how she gets round her little difficulty, then?' observed Mollie with a yawn.

'Shouldn't think there's any question of "getting round it". If the kid has any sense, she'll hold her tongue and do as she's told,' Gillian returned with decision.

'I wonder!' Mollie stretched herself and yawned again. 'Oh, dear! I seem to have a regular fit of the gapes!'

'You'd better ask Matey if you can go to bed early for the next few days,' suggested Gay. 'Why on earth are you so tired just now, Moll? You were trying not to yawn all through science. I saw you sit on it again and again. Aren't you well?'

'I'm all right, thanks. It's just the gapes, as I told you. It's fearfully awkward, though – especially in Bill's lessons. I nearly split my eardrums this morning trying not to in the lab.'

'There *must* be something wrong if you want to yawn all the time,' Gillian said. 'Honestly, Moll, I think you should go to Matey.'

'Oh, no, thank you! I don't believe in rushing headlong on doom!' Mollie retorted. 'You leave me alone, and let's go on with what we were discussing – Which is Verity-Ann's sauce.'

'I don't believe she meant it that way,' said Janet quietly.

'Hello, Jan! Thought you were asleep!' teased Gay.

'I was not, but I hadn't anything to say, so I said nothing. I don't believe in wasting my breath.'

'Regular Scotty, aren't you? Well, go on with what you were saying. Our ears are open to receive any pearls of wisdom you may elect to strew before us – not to say that we are swine, you know.'

'Dry up, Gay!' Jacynth ordered. 'Go on, Jan, and don't mind her. She really can't help it, though it's an awful pity!' And she grinned at the indignant Gay with a grin which transformed her rather sad face.

'Well, if you ask me, I think she's in deadly earnest all the time. I don't think she means to be rude, and I'm glad Joanna didn't report it as such to you, Gill.'

'Well, if you come to that, so am I,' acknowledged Gillian. 'I'd have had to take official notice of it then, and, as you say, Jan, I don't think she means it for cheek. But someone will have to take her in hand some time, or she'll have an awful life of it with the others. Mary-Lou seems to get on like a house on fire with them; but what they can make of Verity-Ann is more than I can tell you. By the way, Mary-Lou seems to be the only one of them who could be called friendly with her.'

'There wasn't much chumminess between them last night,' grinned Nancy. 'If Verity-Ann disapproves of hoydenish games, she must have been disapproving of Mary-Lou with every inch of her. I never heard anything to beat that kid's yells! Foghorns weren't in it!'

69

'But it's so mad!' cried Gay, suddenly becoming serious. 'What right has a kid like that to disapprove of that sort of thing? She ought to be *in* them – up to the eyebrows!'

'Perhaps her people don't approve of games,' suggested Janet. 'What do they consist of – anyone know?'

'Not an idea,' said Nancy airily; but Jacynth struck in, 'Her father is exploring in South America somewhere – Jo Russell told me that much.'

Gillian sat up. 'Did you say South America? I say! I wonder if he's with the Murray-Cameron Expedition? I hope not!'

'Why on earth not?' Gay demanded. 'What's wrong?'

'Why, it was in the papers this morning. They've had no news for ages – about two years, I believe. The people who know think there's been trouble or something. I read the account during our Current Events period, and I remember they mentioned a Commander Carey as the cartographer, and – Oh, my *aunt*!' with deep consternation in her tones, 'they also said that the official entomologist was Professor Trelawney. Anyone know if that's likely to be Mary-Lou's father?'

No one did, but the young faces grew very grave as they realized what the news might mean to their two juniors. There was a short silence broken by another and deeper yawn from Mollie. Thankful for a chance to change the subject, Gay swung round on her. 'Mollie Avery! you're at it *again*!'

'I know,' said poor Mollie, going deeply red. 'I don't seem able to help it.'

A tap at the door heralded the arrival of a Fifth Former who brought a message from Matron. Mollie Avery was to go to her room at once. Lavender withdrew, having delivered her message, and Mollie got off the table and prepared to follow her.

'You're for it!' Gay told her as she left the room.

'I know I am – worse luck!' was Mollie's reply, accompanied by another yawn as she shut the door behind her.

'What do you think is wrong with her?' asked Jacynth. 'Jan, your father's a doctor. Don't *you* know?'

'Dad's being a doctor doesn't make me one!' Janet retorted. 'But, judging by all this yawning, I should say her liver's out of order.'

'Well, thank goodness Matey doesn't approve of castor oil except on very special occasions!' yawned Gay. 'Oh, dear! Mollie must have infected me. What's the time, anyone? Half-past nine? Time we packed up, then. Who's on duty to-night? '

'Me – Frances Coleman – Mollie,' said Gillian after a glance at a big sheet pinned up on the wall by the fireplace. 'You can take her turn, Gay, as Matey's got her in her clutches. I don't suppose she'll let Moll loose for the next day or two. We'd better get going. Tidy up before you go, you folk, and *don't* forget to switch the light off whatever you do. Come on, Gay; we've got to find Frances. Scram!'

The pair left the room, and the rest, after tidying up, also departed for their dormitories with the enigma of Verity-Ann still unsolved.

CHAPTER SEVEN

ENTER CLEM!

By the end of the week it was known all over the school that not only Mollie Avery, but Gay Lambert, Frances Coleman, and Jacynth Hardy were down with jaundice. By the end of another, quite half the members of the three Sixth forms had joined them, and two or three from the Fifths followed suit. When it got to this stage, Miss Annersley quarantined the Seniors, since they seemed to be the only ones affected, and the rest of the school managed without prefects for the next fortnight, by which time half-term was looming into sight.

71

The first two or three weeks of the term had been fine and sunny, but the last ten days had made up for that with heavy storms of rain and great gales. On three separate days neither Mary-Lou nor the Triplets were able to get to school, and Gran informed Mother that something must be done about it. Being Gran, she acted promptly, and the result was that, three days before the week-end began, Mary-Lou was told that when it ended she was to go back to school as a boarder for the rest of that term and the whole of the next.

'A boarder?' she said blankly. 'But why?'

'Because it won't do for you to miss your lessons on account of the weather,' Gran returned.

Mother chimed in: 'Auntie Jo tells me that her three will be boarders till the end of the Easter term too, dear, so you wouldn't have them to play with, even if you stayed at home. Miss Wilson has promised that you may have a week-end at home each half-term, and I shall be able to come up and see you sometimes. It won't be so bad as if you were far away. Cheer up, darling! There are only another six weeks after half-term, and they will pass very quickly.'

'But I'll have to sleep in a room with other people, whether I like them or not,' objected Mary-Lou.

'Yes; but think of the fun you'll have sleeping with other girls. You will be sure to find one or two of your special friends in the same dormitory,' said Mother soothingly, not knowing just how crowded the Chalet School was that term.

'I don't think it'll be *fun*,' said Mary-Lou severely. 'I prefer to be alone at night. It's more private, and I *like* to be private.'

Gran, who was sitting by the fire with her embroidery, cast a despairing look at her grand-daughter. 'At *your* age! What next, I should like to know!'

'But you will have your own cubicle, dear,' said Mother. 'That will make it private in most ways.'

'They're only curtains. Besides, I don't b'lieve there's a

bed to spare in any of the Junior dormies. I've heard Jo
Russell say they're full up this term. It would be simply
ghastly to sleep with a lot of big girls – all on the look-out
to squash you if you only breathe!'

'I don't think it will — ' The telephone rang. Mother
got up and went to answer it, leaving Mary-Lou and Gran
alone.

Gran looked at Mary-Lou. 'You be thankful for curtains, Miss! When *I* was at school, there were twelve of us
in beds, with just enough space between the beds for us to
get up. And I remember your great-grandmother telling
me that in *her* day they had to share beds – not just rooms.
How would you like that, eh?'

'Not at all,' said Mary-Lou promptly. 'I'd hate it!'

'Then be thankful for your cubicle, and don't worry
your mother by whining over what can't be helped. You're
too big to be such a baby now,' said Gran sharply.

Luckily Mother came back smiling at that moment.
She took her small daughter by the shoulders and shook
her gently, crying gaily, 'I've news for you, Mary-Lou!
That was Miss Annersley, and she rang up to tell me that
every dormitory is full this term so they are making a new
one for you and a new girl. And she's only thirteen, so
that's hardly a big girl, is it? *Now* aren't you happier?'

Mary-Lou flung out her hands in exact imitation of
Mlle Berné when someone was being outrageously stupid
over grammar or translation. 'That's worse than all! A
stranger! I shall hate her!'

'You'll do nothing so wicked and un-Christian!' Gran
retorted. 'And stop waving your hands about in that silly
fashion! Where you pick up all these tricks is beyond
me!'

Mary-Lou let her hands drop. Her jaw squared, but
she said no more. What was the use? Mother *couldn't*
and Gran just *wouldn't* understand. But she groused long
and bitterly to her own clan when she saw them next day.

'It *is* bad luck,' agreed Vi Lucy, her dimpled face becoming as long as a round, rosy little face could. 'I wish

73

you could have been in our dormy. We've got that silly ass Celia James, who cries at the least little thing. It's horrid, 'cos everyone thinks we bully her, and we've got into awful rows over it.'

'As if *we* would bully!' Doris Hill chimed in, deep scorn in her voice. 'We aren't cads, I hope! But if you only tell Celia not to be an idiot she squalls! I b'lieve she just does it to get people to fuss over her – little beast!'

From which it will be seen that Celia James had contrived to rouse their worst feelings.

Josette shook her head. 'She's *awful*! It's like having a shower-bath going all the time.'

'Would Matey let us change, d'you think?' asked Mary-Lou hopefully. 'I'll ask her shall I?'

They promptly squashed this idea. 'Goodness, no! Don't you do any such thing. Matey would only think you a fusser, and she loathes fussers,' said Josette earnestly.

'Besides,' added Doris, 'Matey put Celia there, and there she'll stay till she's a Middle – unless she leaves or anything,' she added vaguely.

'And it would put Matey's back up and there's no use in doing *that*,' Vi added her quota. '*We'll* just have to put up with her, and *you'll* have to do the best you can with the new girl. But it's horrid bad luck.'

They had to leave it at that, for the bell rang for afternoon school and Miss Davidson was expecting them in the art-room. They grabbed their pencil-boxes and paints, Josette took the register, and they all hurried off to the big, light room, where they were set down to drawing sprays of blackberries in pastel.

When Thursday came, Mary-Lou bade good-bye to the rest of her form and set off for home in very low spirits. However, Friday brought a tea-party at Plas Gwyn, the Maynard home, and this helped to cheer her up, though 'Aunty Jo' was completely unsympathetic when Mary-Lou tried to unload her woes to her.

'Don't be such a little ape, Mary-Lou,' she said. 'You've got to take the rough with the smooth like everyone else, and whining won't get you anywhere. And to make up your mind beforehand to dislike the poor creature who's got to share a room with you is too jolly unfair for words! Give the poor thing a chance, and stop being such a little moke!'

It was impossible for Mary-Lou to be vexed with Auntie Jo. She turned very red, but that lady was looking at her with black eyes dancing with suppressed mirth, and now held out her hand.

'Come along, old lady! We'll forget all about it and go and play "slides", shall we? I've cleared the drawing-room on purpose.'

'Slides' was a glorious game, and one allowed on especial occasion only. The drawing-room floor at Plas Gwyn was parquet, kept well polished by the faithful Anna. On this occasion, all the rugs had been rolled up, the furniture set back against the walls, breakables put away in safe places, and the wide expanse of the floor – Plas Gwyn was an old house with very large rooms – was clear for a bevy of small girls to sit on thick old mats and push themselves round and round in every direction. There were only two rules: you must wear carpet slippers provided by the hostess; and you *must* wear your very oldest frock, for it was a game calculated to make you hot and dirty, as well as giving a high polish to the parquet. As you frequently collided with other people, it was also an exceedingly noisy game – and all the more fun for that.

They enjoyed themselves thoroughly, and all stood in much need of their hot baths that night. But, as Mary-Lou said to her rather horrified mother, 'I'm not the only one. You should see the Trips and Jo Russell!'

On Saturday Mary-Lou had a party of her own with the Maynards and Russells, and Vi Lucy and Doris Hill. Mother and Gran provided a lovely tea and kindly left them alone to play as they liked in the morning-room, which had been emptied for the occasion. It wasn't quite the rowdy affair the Plas Gwyn one had been, but they made enough noise for Gran to look at Mother as they sat in the drawing-room and say thankfully, 'It's a mercy we don't give a party every day!'

On Sunday, which was fine, Auntie Jo called for Mary-Lou after dinner, and took her off for the rest of the day. Gran hadn't seemed well for the last day or two, and Jo Maynard knew all there was to know about the Murray-Cameron Expedition. She thought that Mother looked as if she needed a rest just now. Later on, if things had really gone badly, Mary-Lou would be her best comfort; but just now, while she was bearing the terrible strain of the anxiety, it was as well to keep the small girl out of the tense atmosphere as much as possible, decided Jo. She kept Mary-Lou until seven o'clock, when 'Uncle Jack Maynard' took her home, and seized the opportunity to see Gran. He diagnosed a coming cold, ordered the old lady off to bed, and advised keeping Mary-Lou out of her room.

This was easy, for on Monday they all went to the Round House for the day. The weather, which had cleared up on Saturday, remained fine, and they were dispatched to play in the patch of woodland near the house. They elected to be Red Indians, and the noise of their yells and war-hoops startled the crows which nested in the woods. They carried off Ailie, the four-year-old Russell baby, to be a white 'papoose', and small Charles Maynard for another.

'They do think of the maddest things to do!' said Lady Russell when she was alone with her sister. 'I only wonder they didn't kidnap your Michael as well! I must say you seem to take it all very coolly, Jo.'

'When you've a crowd like mine – and all so close together – you have to, or die of worry!' retorted her sister, as she fenced Baby Michael in on the settee with many cushions. 'Use your wits, Madge! They won't kill themselves – but I advise you to see that the furnace is kept going, for they'll need a *sea* of baths, I should imagine! Their clothes don't matter. They've all got *rags* on – I saw to that with my crowd; and *where* you resurrected the

76

garments your own daughters are wearing is a mystery to me.'

Madge Russell laughed ruefully. 'I did so hope to have *one* quiet, gentle little girl, but Ailie shows every sign of being the worst of the lot. I must say I think I've had my share of imps, what with you as a kiddy, and now my own.'

'Never mind,' said Jo consolingly, as she left her baby and came to squat on the floor with a pile of darning. 'Oh, *drat* these socks! I don't believe Jack has a single whole heel to his name.'

Madge chuckled. 'Jem bursts out at his toes. Give me a pair and I'll help you.'

'Thank goodness!' Jo spoke fervently. 'I hoped you'd say that. Here you are – and here's the wool to match.'

'And now,' said Madge when they had both settled down to their tasks, 'what's the latest news?'

'What about? Do you mean at the Trelawney's? Nothing yet; but Doris Trelawney is terribly anxious. She says precious little, but I can see she's losing hope. It's been so long since anything came through.'

'How is Mary-Lou taking the idea of being a boarder?' Madge asked after a minute's silence. She said nothing about the Murray-Cameron Expedition, for there was nothing to be said as yet.

'Loathes it!' Jo turned thankfully to a change of subject. 'She came miauing to me about it — '

'*Jo!* What a way to put it!'

'It just about describes it, though. She's a queer kid, isn't she? Jolly as they make 'em; and then you come across a sudden snag like this. My lady came over all hoity-toity about not being private at night, if you please. I told her not to be a little moke — Well, why are you mooing like a cow in the last extremities of acute appendicitis?' For Madge had given vent to a groan.

'Your language! Jo, where *do* you pick up your expressions? No one on earth would ever imagine you were

77

married, let alone the mother of a long family! You're just as awful as ever you were!'

'I wonder you don't suggest I should pay a fine,' grinned Jo. 'I suppose you'd like me to talk like that impossible infant Verity-Ann! By the way, Madge, if the Expedition has come to grief, it will affect her as much as Mary-Lou – more, poor babe, for she hasn't a soul left in the world in that case, I believe.'

'You mothered Jacynth Hardy,' said Madge meaningly.

'I did; but I very much doubt if I or anyone else could "mother" Verity-Ann. I should feel as if I were trying to mother my own great-grandmother!'

'Rubbish!' retorted Madge crisply. 'If you felt like it, you'd mother the queen of the Cannibal Islands in case of need. Jem calls you a champion butter-in, and he's right. You always were, and you haven't altered in that respect any more than in your language.' Then she sobered. 'How very dreadful if – if — '

'It mayn't be any real trouble, Madge. Mail may have been held up. It may even have been lost. No one can say what could happen in such a wild country. Best not to think of it – yet. We can't do anything about it until something definite comes through.'

'We can pray,' Madge replied quietly.

'Oh, I do – every night and morning. But it's all we can do.'

Again a silence fell, broken presently by a murmur from Baby Michael, who had roused up and felt it was time someone noticed him. His mother put down her work and soon settled him off to sleep again. When she returned to her darning, it was to speak of something different.

'I wonder what this new kid that's coming will be like? Mary-Lou must bring her to tea at Plas Gwyn.' For no apparent reason she began to giggle. 'What a shock it's going to be! Hello!' as the clock chimed the hour. 'Isn't it time that crew were coming in to seek food? You haven't given them a picnic meal, have you?'

'I have *not*! Do give me credit for a little sense. It's all

78

very well for them to race about in the spinney, but I won't have them sitting down among that wet undergrowth and catching their deaths of cold. Michael's rousing again. You take him to my room and see to him while I ring the bell to bring our young ruffians home.'

Jo nodded. 'Good scheme!' She dropped her work, got up, and stooped over the settee to pick up her bonny boy, who was informing her that he was hungry, and unless he had a meal in short order he was prepared to yell the house down. 'All right, my lad! We'll see about it at once. Come along!' And she carried him off, and up the wide, shallow stairs to her sister's sunny bedroom, where she laid him on the bed for a minute or two.

She had just settled down when she heard a shriek from her sister so full of horror and dismay that she felt sure something particularly outrageous had happened. Michael tied her, however, so she had to content herself with listening eagerly to the sounds that came upstairs. Madge was scolding; she knew that. Clearly no one was killed or hurt.

'But oh, I wish I knew what they've been up to!' she murmured to Michael.

He was too busy to respond; but when he was satisfied, and Jo was able to lay him down in Ailie's old cot, which still stood in her brother-in-law's dressing-room, she only stayed long enough to be sure that he was snug and drowsy, and then she tore downstairs to find herself faced in the hall with the queerest-looking crowd she had ever seen or even imagined!

Every one of them was *brick-red*! Hands and arms and faces and necks were the same awful lurid colour. There were even streaks of it in their hair. As for their clothes, they were splotched and splashed in such a way as convinced the horrified Jo that they were fit for nothing but the nearest ragbag. She stopped stockstill on the fourth stair, and stared at them with eyes which looked ready to fall out of her head.

'*What – on – earth—* ' she gasped.

'You may well ask!' This was Lady Russell at her most stately. 'These wretched children have found a bucket of red ochre and — '

She got no further. Jo collapsed on the stairs and simply screamed with laughter. 'Oh – oh – oh! Of all the little *sights*! Just look at them! And their *clothes*!'

'Yes; *look* at their clothes!' Lady Russell spoke with some bitterness. 'It's all very well laughing, Jo, but what are we to do with them?'

Sobbing with mirth, Jo caught at the banisters and hauled herself to her feet. 'I ho-hope you've any amount of hot water, Madge,' she choked, 'for it strikes me we shall have to *steep* the lot! L-let me look at you all! Mary-Lou Trelawney! What *would* your Gran say if she saw you? Margot, your hair will have to be washed to get it out. Charles, my poor lamb, little did I think what would happen if I let you out of my sight with only Sybs and Bride in charge. As for you, Sybs, you look the worst of the lot with your own ginger mop and a ginger face to complete the colour scheme. Even Len doesn't look quite so awful. Well, we'd better get you all undressed and bathed, I suppose. Madge, you'd best tell Marie to hold back lunch, for we shan't be ready for it for another hour at least. And then suppose you take Ailie and Mary-Lou to your own bathroom while I attend to my trio and Charles in the scullery. Sybs and Bride can fish for themselves in the nursery bathroom. As for clothes, I suppose you can produce something for them to wear. Your own crowd have things here, anyhow. Can you give me something for the girls and Mary-Lou. As for Charles — '

'I have some of David's little things put away. Luckily I had them out the other day, looking them over, so they are well aired. But really, what they all deserve is to be put to bed with dry bread and milk,' said Madge, biting her lips to keep them following Jo's example and shrieking with laughter. 'Ailie, you and Mary-Lou go to our bathroom and wait there till I come to you. Jo, you take your family to the nursery bathroom. Sybs and Bride can use Marie's I know. I've got plenty of things Stephen's size. If we work hard we may be able to get them fit for dinner by two o'clock.'

It was so. At two o'clock a large and somewhat subdued party sat down to a very belated meal. All looked thoroughly scrubbed, and all the children had damp hair. Madge began with a very dignified air, but Jo spoilt it all by continual fits of suppressed giggles as she recalled the shocking sights they had been, and in the end Lady Russell was obliged to relax. Indeed, when the meal was over, and the party had been sent to play in the nursery, while the two ladies retired to the drawing-room, she gave way altogether, lay back in her chair, and shouted in company with her sister.

The party was very much quieter for the rest of the day. Their clothes were all in Marie's big tub, and Marie had told them exactly what she thought of them all. She had been with Lady Russell since long before her marriage, and she did not spare her words. Also, when they were going home, Len, the eldest of the Triplets, looked down at her brick-dyed finger-nails apprehensively and asked, 'What can we do to get it out, Mamma? Matey will say such horrid things to us if she sees them.'

'You should have thought of that sooner,' retorted her mother. 'I expect she'll talk to you four all right. Anna will do her best for you three, I don't doubt. Mary-Lou, ask Mummy to rub cream into your nails when you go to bed, and it may be all right in the morning. Here we are; jump out, Mary-Lou! She's safe and sound, Doris, though I've left her clothes in the wash-tub at the Round House. They'll be coming back sooner or later. She'll tell you the story; I must get home and see this crowd into bed. Good night!' And off she drove, leaving Mary-Lou to make her own explanations.

Mother paid very little attention. She seemed to be miles away, so her small daughter thought. Mary-Lou was bathed and put to bed with very little said to her throughout the whole business. Mary-Lou wondered a little to herself, but she was wise enough to say nothing, and was soon fast asleep. Nor was there much time next morning, for the alarm clock didn't go off, and they overslept. It was a rush to have Mary-Lou ready for half-past eight, when Jo Maynard arrived with the car to take her to school.

'Good-bye, darling,' said Mother, kissing the little girl fondly. 'I'm sure you'll have a good time. Work well, and write to me at the end of the week. You'd better not come home until Gran's cold is better.'

'Good-bye, Mother,' said Mary-Lou, setting her lips firmly. She felt rather choky, but she wasn't going to cry before the Triplets, who were nearly three years younger than she was.

Auntie Jo seemed rather distracted this morning; she drove quickly along the road, up the long avenue, and finally drew up before the great door of the school.

'Side door, Mamma,' said Len reprovingly. 'We aren't let go in at the front.'

'I forgot.' Her mother started the car again, and drove round to the side door, where she decanted them, handed out their cases, and, after kissing them all round, drove off.

Left alone, the four little girls picked up their cases, entered by the side door, and made their way upstairs to the pretty room where Matron was making out a list of first-aid supplies which she required from Armiford. She greeted the quartette briskly, and then got up. 'Len, you are in Ten; Con, you are in Twenty – both of you on this floor. Mary-Lou and Margot, you are on the floor above; Margot in Twenty-nine, and Mary-Lou in Thirty-five with the new girl. She's there already. Trot along, all of you, and empty your cases. The dormitory prefects will show you how to arrange your clothes. I've told the new girl to show Mary-Lou. She came last night. Now be off! It's almost nine o'clock, and Prayers are at half-past to-day, so you'll have to hurry.'

'Mamma said I was to tell you she's coming to see you one day this week, Matron,' said Len properly.

Matron's rather sharp face softened. 'Thank you; I'll be glad to see her. Now run along, all of you!'

They went off, the Triplets rather subdued. They had expected to be together, as they had been all their lives so far, but Matron knew better than that. Len and Con, though on the same floor, were in dormitories at opposite ends of the corridor, and constant visiting would be impossible. The four parted outside the door, and while Len and Con set off in different directions, Mary-Lou and Margot climbed up the next flight of stairs. When they reached the landing, Margot turned to the right.

'The numbers go on along here,' she whispered. 'Come on, Mary-Lou; you're only a few doors farther on than me.'

Lugging a small suitcase, Mary-Lou trudged along at her side. A door opened, and Nancy Canton appeared, on the lookout for the pair. 'You're in my dormy, Margot,' she said, smiling down into the forget-me-not eyes. 'Mary-Lou, your dormy is five doors along on the other side – right at the far end. Run along quickly, and I'll try to come along before Prayers and see how you're getting on. Come on, Margot!'

Margot followed her into the room, and Mary-Lou dragged on down the corridor. She was feeling rather shy for once, and it was quite an effort to open the door with its freshly painted number, and go in. A girl was standing by the window, looking out. Mary-Lou had just time to see that she was tall, with two long pigtails hanging down her very flat back, when she turned, opening her lips to say something.

It was never said. As her eyes fell on Mary-Lou standing there, they widened. Then she sprang forward with a shout, even as Mary-Lou herself dropped her case, and leaped forward with a positive squeal of excitement.

'Mary-Lou! It isn't really *you*!'

'Clem, oh, Clem! What fun! What gorgeous fun! I

never thought the horrid new girl would be you! When did you come? What made Mr. Barras send you here? Where's Tony? Oh, *Clem*!'

For the seemingly impossible had happened. It was – it really and truly *was* Clem!

CHAPTER EIGHT

CLEM'S STORY

NEITHER of the two was much given to embraces but on this occasion they kissed each other warmly. Then Clem, with one eye to Matron, for whom she already felt a healthy respect, went to pick up Mary-Lou's case. She set it on a chair and began unpacking, while Mary-Lou sat down on the floor to change her shoes.

'We'd better begin on this,' said Clem. 'Is this all you have, Mary-Lou? It won't hold an awful lot.'

'No; there's a big case coming up later on, but this has all I'll need for to-day and to-night. Gran's in bed with a cold, and Mother hadn't time to finish some things off. She rang up Miss Annersley and told her. The other will be coming tomorrow by the carrier. Clem, I had no idea you'd come here.'

'Neither had I. But – well – you know what Tony is – little moke! He's terrified of Dad when he gets into one of his rages; but if Tony sees a chance of a good joke, he just goes ahead regardless. Then he has to pay up for it later.'

'Like the crabs and jelly-fish in the paint-box,' said Mary-Lou reminiscently. 'What did he do this time, Clem?'

'You get on with taking off your things and changing your shoes,' said Clem practically. 'Hang your coat up in that cupboard– the hooks on the right side, I've bagged the left. There's a shelf for your hats above them. Oh, about Tony?'

'Yes; do tell me, please. Oh, and how did you like the Hebrides? There are two girls here – twins they are who used to live on an island called Erisay up there. At present, they live with Auntie Jo– I mean Mrs. Maynard. She's next door to us, and the Triplets are here at school. Auntie Madge – that's Lady Russell – really owns the school, and she's her sister,' said Mary-Lou. 'Clem, leave that, and do let's talk.'

'We can talk while we work,' retorted Clem, going on. 'I know a bit about Erisay. It was about ten miles from us, and when Dad tried to get permission to go there to paint, he couldn't. The Admiralty have it, and they're doing something awfully secret there. They don't let anyone land that hasn't an absolute right to be there. It used to belong to the Macdonalds, but they left. I suppose those twins are Macdonalds?'

'Yes – Flora and Fiona. They're very jolly. But go on and tell me about you,' said Mary-Lou, hanging up her coat.

'Oh, it wasn't too bad; but they'd have had to do something about our lessons, even if Tony hadn't played the giddy goat. The only school there was the village school, and they did everything in Gaelic, so that wasn't much use to *us*. But we might have gone on a bit longer if Tony hadn't messed things up as he did. That put the lid on it, though!'

'What did he do?' Mary-Lou stood with her hat in her hand.

'Shove that thing on its shelf, and come and help me. As for what Tony did, he poured custard over Dad's salad. There *was* a scene. It was a dark day, and Dad thought it was salad dressing. He got a good mouthful of it before he knew what it was.' Clem began to laugh at the memory, and Mary-Lou joined in. 'You should have seen his face! I believe he thought he was poisoned for a moment. Then he let out one great bellow, and made for Tony, who just shrieked with laughter. Mums tried to stop him, but Dad got there first. He yanked Tony out of his chair, laid him across his knee, and gave him the worst spanking he's ever had. Tony had to sit on a cushion for the next two days, for Dad really was so mad, he just laid on. When it was over, Mums snatched Tony up, and then she said, "There's been quite enough of this! I'm not going to have Tony treated like this again. It's time they went to school, anyway. They haven't enough to do here to keep them out of mischief, and it's more than time they were beginning to learn something. You can just get to work and find schools for them!" Then she carried Tony away and put him to bed.'

'Oh, poor Tony!' said Mary-Lou sympathetically.

'Yes; I know. But you must admit he'd asked for it,' returned Clem judicially. 'Well, Dad just leapt at the idea. He got one of the fishing-boats to put him across to the mainland next day, and went up to London to some place where they advise you about schools. He fixed up Tony at a good prep school, and decided on here for me. It was just the day term started, and he wanted to get back as soon as he could, or you might have seen him. But he asked the Head to meet him between two trains, so she went to Armiford. If what he says is correct, he simply said, "I'm sending my daughter to you. Teach her what you like, and keep her in order, and send me the bills. When can you have her?" But it wasn't as easy as all that. For once I rather think he had to more or less get down on his knees before she would agree to take me. She said the school was full as it was. But he talked and talked – and lost his train into the bargain – and at last she said she would. I believe Dad thinks if you've got the money to pay you can get what you like just for the asking,' added Clem, whose father, having a private income apart from the sums he made by his art, had never known what it was to want for anything.

'Fancy arguing with *Miss Annersley*!' breathed Mary-Lou, who held both Heads of the school in some awe.

'Dad would argue with a whole covey of Heads if he felt like it. You ought to know *that*!' Clem retorted. 'Well, apart from all that, I had to have uniform, and they had to find someone to bring us to Liverpool, which didn't happen for six weeks. The minister had to come then, so he said he'd bring us if we'd give him our word of honour to do just what we were told, and behave like Christians. He said exactly that! By that time, you see, everyone in the island knew us.' And Clem smiled impishly.

'When was that?' Mary-Lou asked as she shut the last drawer with a bang.

'Saturday. We spent Sunday in Glasgow and came on here yesterday. At least, Mr. McCrae put me on the train for Armiford at Liverpool, but he took Tony to *his* school. A Miss Linton met me and brought me out here in a car – jolly pretty she is, too, and seems a decent sort – and here I am for the next year, at any rate.'

'How do you mean – for the next year?' demanded Mary-Lou. 'Aren't you going home for the hols?'

'Not very likely. The chances are we shouldn't get across – not in December, anyhow. There might be a storm on, and when you get a storm there, it's a *storm*, I can tell you!'

'Then where's Tony's school if you couldn't come farther than Liverpool together?'

'In Lancashire, up on the moors. It's called Craven House and there are about seventy other boys. He'll stay there till he's old enough to go to public school, I suppose.'

'But – how are you going to see each other?'

'I've no idea. It doesn't look like being this side of Easter, anyhow. Not unless Mums comes across and takes rooms somewhere. But I don't think she'll do that. She never likes to leave Dad for more than a few days at a time. He's such a helpless creature when it comes to cooking and keeping the place comfortable,' said Clem, in the elderly way which had always made Mary-Lou gasp. 'Oh well, we'll just have to grin and bear it. We all knew Dad would come to the end of his tether some day and blow up completely. He can't help it, I think; it's the way he's

87

made. And Tony certainly *asked* for all he got, as I told you before.'

'Well, anyhow, this is a jolly nice school,' said Mary-Lou. 'I'm ever so glad you've come, Clem. It will be such fun being at the same school.'

Clem, busily sorting handkerchiefs in their sachet, did not reply for a moment. Then she said, 'Which form are you in?'

'Upper Second A. Which are you?'

'Upper Third, A division. How many forms are there between us?'

'Lower Third and Upper Third B. But I may get a remove to Lower Third next term if only I can manage my sums. Miss Linton said so when we broke up for half-term. Then there'd be only one form in between us. But oh, Clem! If you're in *Upper* Third *any* division of it – you're Middle school. Lower Third is top of the Junior school. Upper Third B is lowest form in Middle School. You're not a Senior till you're in Lower Fifth. We shan't be much together after all!' And Mary-Lou looked ready to cry.

'Yes; it'll make a bit of difference, I expect. Still, we're sleeping together, so we'll see something of each other that way,' said Clem thoughtfully. Then she changed the subject. 'What are the Macdonalds like – those twins you said came from Erisay? How old are they, to start with?'

'Oh, big girls – sixteen or seventeen. They're in Upper Five B. They're fun, but they talk awfully funnily sometimes.'

'I know. It iss like thiss, issn't it?' Clem sing-songed her speech as she lengthened the sound of every s, and Mary-Lou chuckled.

'It's a bit like that. Sometimes they use p for b, too. How did you know?'

'Because that's the way most of the folk talk on Inch Carrow when they speak English. Even the minister does it a bit.'

'Is that where you are living?'

88

'Yes; it's rather a jolly place–quite small, with enormous cliffs, covered with seabirds at nesting-time, they say. We haven't seen that, of course. But there are thousands of gulls. There's only one landing-place, and they say *that* isn't safe when there's a south-east gale blowing. It was all right in the summer, but the people told us that in the winter they're often cut off from the mainland for weeks at a time. I wonder how Dad will like that?'

'I should think he'd blow up again if he wants to leave and can't,' suggested Mary-Lou cheerfully.

She shut down the lid of her case. 'Where do I put this thing? It's all done now. I do hope I remembered where everything is. Jo Russell says Matey blows up like anything if you aren't absolutely tidy and keep things in their proper place.'

'Help! That's a bright look-out for me!' ejaculated Clem. 'I've begun all right but I doubt if I manage to go on. Your people did make you put things away, Mary-Lou, so it oughtn't to be so bad for you. But you know what we're like at home.'

'But I just used to shove things into any drawer so long as they were out of the way. Gran said things, of course.'

'More or less the sort of thing I shall do, I expect. Oh, well, it looks as if I should *have* to learn to be tidy.'

'You'll learn a lot more than that. We all have to talk French and German as well as English – quite *as* well, I mean.'

'*What?*'

Mary-Lou explained, adding, 'This is a French day. To-morrow it's English, and German on Wednesday. Then we have German on Thursday, French on Friday, English on Saturday, and on Saturday afternoon and Sunday you can talk what you like.'

'Help!' said Clem again. She paused. Then she looked at Mary-Lou. 'Look here! How do *you* manage? You didn't know a word of either last summer when we were all at Polquenel.'

'I know that. But when you've got to say things over

89

and over again till whoever you're talking to says you're all right, you can't help learning something. I can't talk an awful lot yet, but I can a little. I love French, anyway. German is an awful lot harder.'

'Well, all I can say is that I look like being dumb two-thirds of my time,' said Clem resignedly. 'How awful!'

'You'll soon learn,' said Mary-Lou. 'Truly you will.'

'Mary-Lou, no one yet has ever contrived to teach me more French than "j'ai, tu as, il or elle a," and things like that. Do you really imagine that I can ever learn to *talk* French, let alone German which I loathe and despise?'

'That's what Verity-Ann says,' said Mary-Lou. 'But she can speak a little French, and she's *got* to talk German to the mistresses on German days, whether she likes it or not, though she won't say a word out of lessons.'

'Who on earth is Verity-Ann?'

'A kid in my form. She's queer. She never went to school before – like me. But she doesn't seem to find it so easy to fit in as I do. I love school now, Clem.'

'I always thought you would once you'd got over the beginning. But if she does as you say, I don't wonder she doesn't fit in, as you call it,' said Clem decidedly. 'I'm not going to be classed with anyone as daft as that, so I suppose I'd better dig my toes in and try to learn. I wonder if I can make any sort of fist at it?'

'If I can, you can,' said Mary-Lou. 'You're older'n I am, and you've been at school for years and know the right way to do things. I'd done lots of them wrong, and I've had to learn all new ways – in some things, anyhow. Bother! There's the bell!' as the ringing of a big bell suddenly filled the place.

'What's that for?' asked Clem. 'Prayers – or what?'

'First bell – go to your form-rooms,' said Mary-Lou.

They left the room and found themselves in a stream of girls racing down to their form-rooms. Mary-Lou caught at someone as she ran past with an eager 'Oh, Betsy, this is my chum Clem Barras. She's just come last night, and she's in your form. Will you show her where to go? Clem, this is Betsy Lucy.'

Betsy, a small, slim girl of about twelve or thirteen with a quaintly puckish face and golden-brown hair cut very short, stopped and nodded. 'Right you are! Come on, Clem, and I'll take you down to Miss Slater. She's our form-mistress.'

Clem was hauled away, and Mary-Lou, meeting Vi Lucy – Betsy was the second Lucy girl – tagged on to her, but said no more, for talking was as strictly forbidden in the upper corridors as the lower, and she knew it. In the form-room, however, as Miss Linton was not there, Vi demanded to know who the girl was in her room. 'I s'pose she's in Upper Third A as you shoved her on to Betsy,' she said. 'Who is she?'

'You know that girl I told you about that I was chums with in Polquenel? Well, it's her. Her brother Tony poured custard over their dad's salad, and he was wild with him, so he sent both of them to school. Anyhow, they'd have had to go,' cos they are living on an island in the Hebrides near to where Flora and Fiona used to live, and Clem says the only school on the island was the village school and they didn't speak English – only Gaelic, and she can't speak Gaelic.'

Vi giggled appreciatively over Tony's prank. 'Does Clem do that sort of thing?' she asked.

'No fear! Clem used to spend her time trying to save Tony from being spanked. But she's not priggy a bit. She's awfully good fun,' added Mary-Lou loyally, 'and she could climb like anything. Gran used to say she believed she must be half a goat. You should have seen her go up our cliffs!'

'Well, there aren't any cliffs here, so it won't be much good to her that way,' said Vi practically. 'She looks rather nice, though. But you said you were going to hate the new girl 'cos you had to sleep with her. What'll you do about that?'

'I didn't know it was going to be Clem, though – sh!

91

Here's Miss Linton coming!' And the pair scuttled to their desks and sat down, just as Miss Linton entered with a pleasant 'Bonjour, mes enfants.'

As two-thirds of the form had been gabbling as hard as they could go in English, having conveniently forgotten that this was a 'French' day, several people went red, Mary-Lou and Vi among them. Miss Linton sat down at her desk, looked round, and smiled. She knew all about it.

'From now on you must talk in French for the rest of the day,' she reminded them in that tongue.

This was familiar. They heard it on an average of two out of every three 'French' days. But her next remark required translation.

'Ce semestre, on va chanter pour unconcert à Noël, et nous allons apprendre les cantiques de Noël. Après nos Prières, Lesley, il faut aller à la salle de papeterie, et demander à Frances des cahiers pour copier les cantiques.'

They looked at each other. What did all this mean? Miss Linton patiently repeated her speech three times, and then called on Vi Lucy to 'traduisez, s'il vous plaît.'

Rising to her feet, Vi mumbled something about Christmas. 'But I don't know what "semest" – I mean,' as she caught the eye of the mistress, 'je ne sais pas "semestre" or – ou "cantiques".' Then, with an air of relief, 'Je n'en comprehends' – a sentence which Upper Third A could all use, since they needed it a dozen times a day. And they were by no means the only form who were obliged to confess ignorance of at least half that was said to them in French. It was being a tough job to get the school at large to talk French; but the Staff all stuck to it with vim, and, as a whole, they were improving.

' "Cantiques de Noël" est le français pour "Christmas carols",' said Miss Linton encouragingly.

'Thank you – I mean, merci beaucoup,' said Vi in a hurry. Then she managed to translate: 'This term one goes to sing for a – a — '

' "Concert," ' prompted Miss Linton smilingly.

'Tha – merci beaucoup – for a concert to Christmas, and

we go to learn some Christmas carols. After our Prayers, Lesley, you must go to the room of – of — '

' "Stationery," ' quoth Miss Linton curtly. 'Continuez!'

'Merci – of stationery, and ask to Frances — '

'Non, Viola. En français il faut dire "à demander à," mais pas en anglais.'

Thus brought up short, Vi lost her head and stood with her mouth opening and shutting like a stranded codfish. Miss Linton was a merciful person, however.

'Asseyez-vous,' she said with a smile; and Vi thankfully sat down.

Mary-Lou, called on to wind up her chum's very lame translation, glibly repeated, 'Lesley, you must go to the stationery room and ask Frances for some exercise-books to copy the carols.'

'Très bien, Mary-Lou,' said Miss Linton, feeling grateful for at least *one* pupil who had taken to French conversation like a duck to water; and Mary-Lou sat down both feeling and looking smug over her success.

Meanwhile, at least half a dozen people were dying to ask questions, but were unable to do so as their French was unequal to the strain. Miss Linton produced her register, however, took it, and then, as there was still time, sat back, and, speaking very slowly, and repeating her phrases till they had got the gist of what she was saying, told them in French that instead of the usual Christmas play they were to give a carol concert this year, and would begin to learn the carols at once. By the time they had gathered this the bell was ringing for Prayers, so they formed their lines and marched off, glad as usual that Prayers, at any rate, were in their own language.

Mary-Lou glanced behind when she was in her place, to see Clem standing between Betsy Lucy and Sybil Russell, and looking quite happy. Clem gave her small friend a beaming smile, but there was no chance of speaking, of course, and once they had marched out to lessons, no hope of seeing each other before Break. However, when they had dispatched their milk and biscuits, Mary-

Lou made a bee-line for Clem, who welcomed her with a wild effort at French.

'Oh, Mary-Lou, savez-vous talker en français comme ça?' For the stunned Clem had had a glimpse of Mary-Lou carrying on an argument with Josette Russell in the kitchen where they had their 'elevenses'. 'Je know nothing de elle.'

'Français est masculin, vous chèvre!' retorted Mary-Lou – to be brought up short by Mollie Avery, who happened to pass them in time to overhear her call the new girl 'you goat' in French. So she said very firmly, 'Mary-Lou, ce' n'est pas gentille à parler comme ça! Ne le répétez encore!' and went on, hoping devoutly that her own French would pass muster.

Mary-Lou went very red; but when the prefect had gone, she grinned at Clem, who couldn't understand a word.

'Que dit-elle?' asked Clem anxiously.

'Elle a dit que ce n'est pas gentille de moi – that means I'm not polite – à vous nommer une chévre,' returned Mary-Lou. 'It means "goat",' she added for the benefit of her less learned friend. 'I said you were a goat. That's all. – Voilà tout!' For Jacynth Hardy was approaching.

Clem sighed heavily. 'Je ne pense pas how you do it!'

'Oh, c'est bien facile,' replied Mary-Lou, who had every reason for knowing this speech, since she heard it a good many times every 'French' day. 'Il faut écouter, et répéter, et alors on apprit très tôt.'

Clem was lost in admiration of her, not knowing yet that this was a favourite remark with Miss Edwards, and Mary-Lou had merely picked it up parrot fashion.

'Savez-vous write en français aussi?' asked Clem carefully.

Mary-Lou went red again. 'C'est plus facile à parler qu'il est à écrire,' she admitted. Her written French was still far from satisfying Mlle Berné, as she very well knew.

The bell for the end of Break separated them, and they parted, Mary-Lou to struggle with Dictée from Mademoiselle; and Clem to enjoy a gym lesson, where she soon proved that, whatever her shortcomings in French, she was a born gymnast. All her movements were clean and quick; her jumping was light and in good style; and she went up the rope like a monkey, coming down hand over hand as expertly as a sailor.

'If only the lesson had been in English,' she told Mary-Lou in the queer, polygot mixture she was contriving to employ at present, 'I'd have enjoyed it from beginning to end. Thank goodness there were three or four people in front of me who knew more or less what Miss Burn meant, and I was able to do what they did! So it wasn't too bad after all.'

'Taisez-vous, Clem. Si les prefects nous entendent, il y aura un *row*,' replied Mary-Lou, most of Clem's speech having been, perforce, in English.

German day was worse. Clem knew a few French phrases, and various verb tenses by heart, so she had been able to manage after a fashion, and Mary-Lou had given her all the help she could out of lesson hours. But of German the elder girl knew not a word, and Mary-Lou was not so quick in picking it up, so their remarks to each other were both bald and brief. But next day was 'English' day, and they made up for it then, like everyone else.

'There's only one thing for it,' said Clem, during the evening when they were getting ready for bed. 'I'll just *have* to learn if it *busts* me to do it. I'm not going to make a moke of myself like that silly little ass of a Verity-Ann!'

On the days when she had to speak German in lessons, whether she liked it or not, Verity-Ann had remained dumb during all Break or free time. Her talk with Miss Annersley had brought her no respite from the hated language; and an impassioned letter on the same subject to her grandfather's solicitor had only given her a reply which said that she must make the most of her opportunities, which were greater than those in an ordinary boarding-school, and be thankful for them.

Thankful, indeed! Verity-Ann considered that she was one of the most ill-used girls in the land, and had fully made up her mind that when her father *did* come home she would appeal to him with all her strength to be allowed to give up *all* languages but her own! However, since it had to be at present, she managed to learn enough to pass muster. But use German when it wasn't a mistress to whom she *must*, she would not. And since she disliked being penniless, she simply became dumb on 'German' days during their free time, and refused to say anything, good, bad, or indifferent.

CHAPTER NINE

A VERY BAD PLAN!

CLEM soon settled down. She had been to various schools before, and knew more or less what was expected of her. In addition, she was a philosophical young person, who took life very much as it came, and did not fret over what could not be helped. She missed Tony terribly, and if it had not been for Mary-Lou she might even have been unhappy, for it was the first time since his birth that they had been separated, and she was one of those people who must have someone to look after. But Mary-Lou was there, so she 'took her on', as she said herself, in place of Tony. Besides this, she made friends – Sybil Russell, Betsy Lucy, and Primula Venables all found in her a kindred spirit. Sybil and Betsy were as wild as she was, and Primula, a tiny, slender girl, with a primrose mop of fine silky hair and big blue eyes, found that the new girl was as great a nature-lover as herself. So during school-hours she and Mary-Lou saw very little of each other. Not that there was much time for either of them to be together. Mary-Lou had made up her mind to work hard and gain her remove at Christmas; and as Vi Lucy, Lesley Malcolm, and Doris Hill had no mind to be left behind by a girl who had just come that term, the four of them managed to set a fashion in hard work which pulled up the form's average considerably.

'You are mean to slog like this, Mary-Lou!' wailed Josette on one occasion. 'However hard *I* work, they'll never move me up at Christmas. I'm under age for this form, and some of the girls in Lower Third are *twelve*, and they'd never let a girl of nine go there.'

'I don't see why not if she can do the work,' said Mary-Lou, standing surveying her with her hands on her hips in a way that Gran would have called most unladylike.

'They'd say the work was too hard for me or something silly like that. They've always fussed ever since I was scalded when I was a small kid. And it's so mad, 'cos I'm as fit as anyone now. But they *will* do it! You know they do yourself.'

'But you'll be ten by Christmas. *Aren't* you ten very soon?'

'Next week. The Triplets and Auntie Jo and I are all in November. When Ailie came, I heard Uncle Jack tell Daddy that he was thankful she hadn't chosen to be two months later or the family cash couldn't have stood the strain of so many birthdays. The Triplets' birthday was a fortnight ago, and Auntie Jo's is next week like mine. I'm the twenty-third, and she's the twenty-seventh, so there's just four days between.'

'Well, Vi isn't eleven till January, and I'm not till June. I know Lesley and Doris are both eleven now, but it's only just. Their birthdays were both last month.'

'No: but Vi will be *almost* eleven when we come back after Christmas, and you'll be ten and a half. I shall be just ten and six weeks, and it makes a difference – or they think it does. I wish you'd slack off a bit, or we shan't be in the same form, and I shouldn't like that.'

'Look here,' said Mary-Lou, putting an arm round Josette's shoulders, 'you just try – I don't mean slog till you're ill, but just work steadily. You've done awfully well so far. You are the youngest girl in the form, and you

D

always are well up in the lists, and you might do it all right. Anyhow, even if you don't, you'll get all the prizes if we four go up. Verity-Ann might beat you in some things; but she won't try in French or German – silly moke! – and her arith's worse than mine, so she hasn't a chance for form or exam prize. If we four move up, you'd get both with a bit of luck.'

Josette looked doubtful. 'I might get *one*; but you never know with Verity-Ann. She's so awfully queer!' Which was her way of saying what everyone felt – that Verity-Ann Carey was a very dark horse indeed.

Still, having never fallen below sixth in the weekly form lists for the first half of the term, Josette had no intention of dropping lower, so she, too, worked hard. She had one advantage over Mary-Lou. She had been taught on modern lines from the very first, and had had nothing to unlearn. And, Sybil to the contrary, she was a clever little thing with a good memory.

But Mary-Lou felt herself at a disadvantage in certain subjects. She had made up her mind to grasp new methods in arithmetic as soon as she could, and began to pester Clem to show them to her. Clem, a good-natured girl, was nothing loath. All the Juniors went to bed at eight, and lights-out came for them at a quarter to nine to allow bath people to be back in their cubicles before that.

Mary-Lou begged Clem to hurry to bed and did the same herself so as to be ready when that young lady came up at half-past eight, and then, until lights-out for Clem, the pair worked hard at problems on compound rules, very simple fractions, decimals, and areas and practice. At least half an hour every night after they were safe in bed was given by the pair to sums, and Miss Edwards found herself awarding sevens and eights to the new girl in place of the ones and twos which had been the rule at the beginning of term.

What neither Mary-Lou nor Clem could understand was that you cannot go on working your brain hard during the proper hours for lessons, and then do the same thing last thing at night, without paying for it. Mary-Lou began to find that when the prefect on duty had said good night and switched off the light, it was a difficult thing to get to sleep. She tossed and turned, and tried counting sheep going through a gate, or repeating mentally all the poetry and tables she had ever learnt but that seemed to make no difference. And when she did drop off at last, it was generally to irritating dreams of sums that simply *wouldn't* come out, no matter how hard she tried. In her sleep she worked pages and pages full of figures, every line getting longer and longer, and every sum getting more and more complicated but she never got the right answer.

Her face began to show it. Her cheeks were losing their roses, and her eyes looked heavy after one of these unrefreshing nights. Matey noticed, of course – 'Trust Matey!' as Jo Maynard would have said – and promptly dosed her. But the dose didn't seem to do much good. Clem was less badly affected, for she was not working nearly so hard as her small friend during the day, and, apart from this, was of a far more placid nature. But even she began to have nightmares, and on one or two nights she flatly refused to do anything, alleging that she was far too tired. Finally, both of them were as cross as two sticks during the day.

'I simply can't make out what's wrong with that Mary-Lou child,' said Matron one evening when she was sitting with Miss Annersley and Miss Wilson in the library, enjoying a well-earned rest with some delicious coffee. 'She always looks tired out, and I'm sure she's sleeping badly. I went in late one night last week, and she was muttering away in her sleep as hard as she could go. I thought it might be tummy trouble, so I gave her a dose; but it doesn't seem to have had much effect.'

'She's not homesick, is she?' asked Miss Annersley in some concern.

'I don't think so. She was happy enough the first week or so after half-term. I heard Vi Lucy telling her she was like a bear with a sore head this morning. There must be some reason for it. I should have said she was a sweet-tempered little soul as a rule.'

'She's working very hard,' said Miss Wilson thoughtfully. 'In geography she's practically level with the rest of the form now. And so far as the map of Europe is concerned, she can point to any country you like to name, which is a good deal more than most of them can. Lesley Malcolm calmly told me the other day that Albania was the capital of Norway! I nearly slew her. I don't even know what the little ass meant, or where she got it from! I soon disillusioned her, I may say. And some of the others aren't any better. There's quite a lot to be said for some of the old-fashioned methods of teaching, you know.'

'Oh, I know,' Miss Annersley agreed. 'I believe in mingling the old *and* the new – making the best of both, in fact. But to get back to Mary-Lou. Suppose we send for Gillian and Dollie – after all, they have most to do with her in school – and see what they think?'

'Well, we must do something,' rejoined Matron crisply. 'The child isn't well, and I want to know why.'

Miss Annersley rang the bell, and when the maid appeared, asked her to tell the two young mistresses they were wanted in the library.

'And bring some more cups, please,' she added, rising.

'Going to make fresh coffee?' Miss Wilson queried. 'Well, I could do with another cup. It's quite an idea.'

By the time the pair had arrived, the percolator, set on a gas ring also in the cupboard, was nearly boiling. Miss Annersley pushed forward comfortable armchairs before the fire, and supplied everyone with coffee and chocolate biscuits before she opened fire. When everyone was served, however, she went straight to the point by saying, 'I've sent for you two to ask you a few questions about Mary-Lou Trelawney. Matey says she isn't sleeping well, and she certainly doesn't look very fit just now. Can you explain it?'

'Why?' asked Miss Linton, wide-eyed. 'What's she been doing?'

'That's what I want to know. What have you to report?'

'So far as I'm concerned, nothing out of the way. She's a monkey, of course, but not more so than a dozen others I could name – Josette and Vi, for instance. *And* Lesley and Doris. Oh, and several more. You don't get baby angels in any Second Form that I've ever had any dealings with!'

'She's improving in arithmetic,' said Miss Edwards. 'She always knew her tables as far as she'd gone, and her methods are really up to date now, thank Heaven! I've had a thin time of it with her and Verity-Ann Carey. *She's* no better, of course. Funny little thing!'

'Do you mean funny-peculiar, or funny-haha?' asked Miss Wilson with interest.

'Funny-peculiar, of course. There's nothing very comic about Verity-Ann that *I've* ever found.'

'Mary-Lou is making tremendous headway in my subjects,' said Gillian Linton. 'If you come to that, the whole form are working splendidly. I never had such a form of workers before. Really, Miss Annersley, I meant to ask you if you thought it would do to give Mary-Lou, Lesley Malcolm, and Vi Lucy their removes after Christmas? Doris Hill is also a possibility. She isn't quite so clever as the other three – I really do think that trio will do something for us later on – but she does work, and she has improved amazingly.'

'What do you think, Dollie?' asked Miss Wilson.

'Vi and Lesley for my subjects. Doris could get through with a push. And Phil Craven isn't too bad — '

She was interrupted by a shriek of horror from Gillian.

'My dear girl! Phil Craven can't spell to save her life; her reading is awful; and her so-called French and German make Julie Berné's hair stand on end! She can't manage more than half a page on *any* subject you like to set them for compo, and her ideas on history are simply *wild*! You *can't* put a child like Phil Craven up. Bracey would have our blood!'

The two Heads and Matron sat back to let the pair

battle it out between them. They felt that they might learn a good deal from the chatter of their two juniors.

'Phil Craven is miles ahead of Vi Lucy in arithmetic,' argued Miss Edwards. 'If you put Vi up, you ought to put Phil up. And certainly if you put Mary-Lou and Doris up it would be most unfair to leave Phil down. She can make rings round those two when it comes to sums!'

'Every one of the other three can read well their spelling is quite good for small girls; they can express themselves well on paper – Vi has a real gift that way – and their French is good and their German coming on. You can't say a single thing that way for Phil Craven. The only one that's worse at German than she is is Verity-Ann Carey, and I'm certain that is only because the little wretch won't try to learn. She could do it well enough if she chose to give her mind to it, for her French isn't too bad now.'

Miss Annersley permitted herself a chuckle. 'She doesn't approve of German, my dear. I suppose you know that?'

'She told me so the very first day of term – after Bill had dropped her bombshell on us – cheeky brat! No; I take that back. There's nothing cheeky about Verity-Ann. Mary-Lou could be cheeky if she liked, I should think. But not in my wildest flights of imagination could I see Verity-Ann any other than painstakingly polite!'

Miss Edwards suddenly laughed.

'What's the joke?' demanded Miss Wilson sternly.

'Just that one day last week I'd been – well – I'm afraid you could only call it "nagging" at Mary-Lou about her area sums. They do very simple ones, you know – just length multiplied by breadth in feet, and give the answer in square yards – things like that. Or yards, and give the answer in square feet. She was a little slow in grasping it – maths is definitely *not* her subject! – and I had got up cross, and lost my temper with her. To finish the lesson and give them a breather, I turned on to Mental for the last ten minutes. I asked "shot" questions – you know –

give them something quite easy, and expect the answer by return of post, so to speak. We had been doing mental addition – seven and nine; eight and five and so on; Mary-Lou made two or three boss shots, and I finally snapped at her, "Two and six – see if you can tell me what that is!" The imp beamed at me, and answered, "Half a crown!" I nearly ate her when I got my breath back. But luckily for her, the bell went just then, and I had to let them go as it was gym. But I gave the lady a jolly good talking-to later on, for it was downright cheek and she meant it for cheek.'

Her auditors were in fits of laughter.

'Oh, Dollie – Dollie- To ask her a question like that!' said Miss Wilson, wiping the tears of mirth from her eyes. 'My dear girl, you simply *asked* for it! Well done, Mary-Lou!'

Miss Edwards flushed. 'Oh, I should have kept my temper, I know. But you don't know, Nell, how utterly maddening Mary-Lou had been that morning. But on the whole I must admit that she has made astonishing progress lately.'

'She was third in last week's form list, bracketed with Doris and Josette,' said Miss Linton. 'Vi was top and Lesley second. Phil was right down in the 'teens – somewhere about fourteenth or fifteenth, I think. And she wouldn't be *there* if it weren't for your marks, Dollie.'

'Vi won't be top this week,' observed Miss Wilson. 'Not unless she has done wonders in other subjects, that is. She forgot to give in her last two exercises, and as they're all corrected and marked, *and* the marks entered, I gave her nought. And she got muddled in her spot test this morning, and has presented me with some really extraordinary information. Wait a moment. I have their papers here.'

She got up and went over to her desk at the other side of the room, whence she fished out a bundle of papers, pulled out the last sheet, and began to read aloud. ' "A volcano is a mountain that is sometimes sick".'

'*What*?' exclaimed Miss Annersley.

'That's what she says, anyway.'

'How simply marvellous!' Miss Linton was giggling like one of her own charges. 'Any more like that, Bill?'

'Plenty! I can't think where her wits can have been. Just you listen to this! "Etna is a meths stove." And here's another: "Wind is something you can feel but not see. It is caused by holes in the air." But she said one thing rather neatly, I thought. I asked them to explain the difference between weather and climate. They have a formula for it, of course. This is Vi on the subject. "Weather may be but climate is." '

'Jolly well expressed!' said Gillian Linton fervently.

'You're side-tracking,' said Miss Annersley, waving her percolator. 'Any more coffee, anyone? It'll just run to another cup each, I believe – Gillian, what about Mary-Lou? Matron is worried about her, and from what you two say I'm inclined to believe that — '

She got no further. At that moment the door was flung open dramatically, and Clem Barras, clad in a green dressing-gown, her feet bare, and her long red-brown hair worked loose from its bedtime ribbon and flying about her in a perfect banner, appeared before them.

'Oh, please someone come to Mary-Lou!' she cried. 'She's wide awake, and talking the most awful rot – all about sums! And I can't get her to stop though I've tried! Do, please come!'

'Clemency! My dear child!' exclaimed Miss Annersley, dropping the percolator and jumping up from her chair, while Matron bounded out of hers and made for the door even as the much-tried Clem forgot her usual, half-grown-up ways, and became merely a badly frightened and unhappy little girl who dissolved into tears as the Head's kind arms went round her, and wailed, 'Oh, it's all my fault! I shouldn't have let her try to do it! It's all my fault, and now she's ill with it!'

Miss Wilson ran after Matron, and the two junior mistresses discreetly melted from the room, leaving Miss Annersley to deal with the weeping Clem, which she did by drawing her to the fire and making her sit down beside her on the big settee. 'Now, Clemency, don't cry like this. Mary-Lou probably has a little fever, and needs some of Matron's cooling mixture. She will be all right in a day or two. I expect. Stop crying and try to tell me what you two have been doing that you ought not. I'm sure it isn't anything very bad.'

It took Miss Annersley some time to calm Clem to the point where she could do anything but sob loudly; and even then it was difficult to understand what she said. Between her remorse and her howls, it was just as well that the Head was a patient woman wso understood girls. But at length the whole story was out, and Clem, greatly relieved now that she had made a clean breast of it, was sitting with her eyes red and swollen, and occasional gulps still shaking her, but calm on the whole.

'It was very silly of you,' said the Head, when she finally understood the whole thing. 'Don't you know, Clem, that the human brain can only absorb so much knowledge at a time, just as your legs can walk only a certain distance, or your tummy take only a certain amount of food? If you over-walk, then your legs are too tired to go on; and if you over-eat, you are sick. It is just the same thing with your brain. If you try to cram too much into it, it goes on strike sooner or later. Now, between you, you and Mary-Lou have been trying to give her brain more than it can deal with at once by working out of proper hours. You have excited it, and so she is feverish and is running a temperature. But it hasn't gone on long enough to hurt her really, which is a very good thing. I shall ask Matron to take her to San for a few days, and then she will be all right again. But remember this. You are never to do lessons, either your own or someone else's, out of the proper hours. And never after eight o'clock at night. When you are a Senior with public exams before you, you may be given permission to work a little later sometimes; but until that comes I want you to promise me that all lesson-books shall be shut at eight at latest. Will you?'

'Oh, I will! I promise you I will!' said Clem fervently.

'That's right! Now I'm going to heat some milk for you, and then I'll take you to bed and tuck you in, and you must try to sleep. Don't worry about Mary-Lou. I expect she'll be quite all right in a few days' time.'

Thus spoken to, Clem was comforted. She sipped her hot milk when it was ready, and then went upstairs accompanied by the Head, who remade her bed for her, saw her into it, and tucked her up with a kiss, and then left her to fall asleep, happier for the kindness and understanding she had been shown, even though Mary-Lou's bed was now empty.

Having seen her well on the way to dreams, Miss Annersley went to San, feeling more worried about Mary-Lou than she had let Clem know. But her worry was needless. Matron's patent mixture was already taking effect, and Mary-Lou was lying quietly, the burning flush not quite so bright, though it was still there and her blue eyes were brilliant.

'Temp at 103 degrees,' said Matron softly. 'However, she's had a dose of my cooling mixture, and I've given her a sponge-down, and in another hour or so she'll have dropped a point or two. There's no rash — '

'Nor likely to be,' interrupted Miss Annersley. 'What do you think those two mad babies have been doing? Working at Mary-Lou's sums after Clem went up to bed. It seems Mary-Lou wants to be moved up after Christmas so as to be as much with Clem as possible, and begged for help. Clem has no more sense than can be expected at her age, and agreed. That's all that's wrong – that, and, I expect, the excitement of school for the first time at her age. Nothing infectious, thank Heaven!'

'Thank Heaven, indeed!' ejaculated Matron. 'Well, if that is all, she can stay where she is for the next few days, and take life quietly. I've sent for Nurse, and she will sleep here with her until the temp is normal. Light diet, bed, and a few days by herself will set her right by Monday, I expect. She's a highly strung child, I should judge;

and that sort always indulges in a temp when it's over-excited. Remember the frights Jo Bettany used to give us? But I hope you've given Miss Clemency a good dressing-down for doing lessons at such a ridiculous hour!'

'There wasn't any need. Of course I've forbidden it, and explained to her where they went wrong. But she was such a heart-broken little object of misery that even you, Matey, would never have found it in your heart to scold her. I made her drink a cup of hot milk and packed her off to bed, and I expect she's asleep by now.'

'I'll just look in on her before I go to bed,' said Matron as Miss Wilson came in with Nurse, who had been in the staff-room at the other side of the house. 'Well, I've had to contend with some queer girls during my years here, but never with one of Mary-Lou's age, anyhow, who made herself ill by overdoing with lessons!'

CHAPTER TEN

'DO YOU THINK ME HORRID?'

FOR the next day or two, Mary-Lou was poorly enough to be glad to be in bed and lie still. She was 'hotty-cold', and her head felt queer. But after that, the temperature went down, and, though still weak from the fever, she felt more like herself, and was able to grasp exactly what had happened. Here she was in bed, losing her marks, and then, perhaps, that coveted remove at Christmas would never happen! Mary-Lou was thoroughly disgruntled. And then Mother never came near her. Was Mother cross with her because she had, as the Head had said, been a silly little girl and broken rules?

Mary-Lou said nothing to the older people about her. If Mother was vexed, then she must tell about it herself. If Gran was, then the youngest member of the Trelawney family knew she would not spare to express herself very firmly. Meantime there were the school people to deal with, and they were quite enough for the moment. But it *was* strange that neither Mother nor Gran had come to see her. Mary-Lou was puzzled.

On the fourth day after that eventful night she tackled Nurse on another subject. 'Nurse, I truly feel all right. Please, càn't I have my lesson-books for a bit? I'm getting all behind, and I don't want to do that.'

'Certainly not!' said Nurse with decision. 'Lesson-books, indeed! You've already been told that the reason why you're here is because you've done far too much with your lesson-books. You can have a story-book if you like when I've finished with you; but you're not going to bother your head with lessons as long as I have any say in the matter.' She finished brushing Mary-Lou's fair hair, and proceeded to plait it in the two plaits tied with ribbons in which it was always worn. It had grown since the summer, and the plaits were now well below Mary-Lou's shoulders. She twitched one of them round to examine it, and then tossed it back. Nurse smiled, and proceeded to pull the little blue woolly closer round her, for it was a cold day.

'Now keep that round you. I don't want you to get a cold on top of everything else, you know. If you're a good girl, you may get up for tea. And if *that* doesn't hurt you, well, I won't promise, but I expect you'll be able to go back into school on Monday. So you won't have lost so very much.

'Nearly all my marks, though,' mourned Mary-Lou.

'Oh, you'll soon make those up again. Here's your Ovaltine and biscuits. Matron sent you ginger snaps to-day for a treat.'

Mary-Lou's face brightened. She loved ginger snaps. When she had disposed of the 'elevenses', Nurse drinking her coffee at the same time, she said, 'Well, if I can't have my lesson-books, can I have a "Lavender" book instead?'

Nurse, who knew what favourites the books were with

the small fry, nodded. 'Yes; I'll go and get it. Which do you want?'

Mary-Lou considered. 'I've read a lot of them now. Jo Russell lent me two or three, besides what I got from the lib'ry. I'm not sure — Oh, I know! May I have *Lavender Laughs in Kashmir*? Jo and Vi told me there's another girl in that who was here for a while.'

'Lilamani,' nodded Nurse. 'Yes; she was here for two years. Then she went back to Kashmir. If it's in, you shall have it. If not, I'll just bring two or three, and you can choose for yourself. Will that do?'

'Yes, thank you,' said Mary-Lou. Suddenly she threw her arms round Nurse as that lady bent to pull the pillows up again. 'You *are* a dear, Nurse. Thanks ever so much.'

'Oh, nonsense!' said Nurse brusquely. 'The sooner you're off my hands, the less work I shall have to do. Now stay quietly till I get back. And for goodness' sake try to keep your bed from looking like an overturned haystack!'

She left the room, and Mary-Lou leaned back against her pillows and gazed out of the window. She couldn't see very much – only the bare tree branches against the pale blue of the December sky. But if she were to get up for tea, that didn't matter now. It was a fine day, so perhaps Mother would come and have tea with her. Supposing she asked Nurse if someone could ring up and ask her? And if Mother wanted to scold, then she would get it over. That was one good thing about both Mother and Gran. Once a sin had been dealt with, it was never mentioned again. She would do it! She would ask Nurse if it would be all right, and then perhaps Nurse would agree.

Nurse herself returned at that moment, bringing with her a visitor – a tall, graceful visitor, clad in a soft green frock, with her black hair, worn with a broad fringe and two thick coils over her ears, uncovered. Mary-Lou sat up.

'Auntie Jo!' she cried. 'How lovely! But where's Mother?'

Jo Maynard nodded at Nurse, who had laid down a

book on the bedside table. 'All right, Nurse. I'll stay with her for a while and you can be free.'

Nurse glanced at her, nodded back, and went out, closing the door quietly behind her. 'Poor little soul!' she thought to herself as she went off to seek Matron.

Meanwhile, Mary-Lou had been kissed and set back against her pillows, and her visitor had sat down on the side of the bed, and was looking at her.

'Well, there isn't much wrong with you that I can see,' she remarked. 'Feel all right?'

'Yes; only a bit woggly when I get up for Nurse to make the bed. But she says that'll soon pass. Auntie Jo, why hasn't Mother or Gran been up to see me? Are they awfully cross with me?'

'No,' said Jo. 'They were upset, of course, when they heard what a little moke you'd made of yourself; but it's forgotten now. Your Gran's not well, and your Mother couldn't leave her.'

'Has she got *another* cold?' demanded Mary-Lou. 'It isn't like Gran. It was always Mother who got the colds before.'

'No; it isn't a cold,' said Jo gently. She leaned back against the pillows, slipping an arm round Mary-Lou, who nestled up against her, nothing loath. Jo looked down at the little shining head against her shoulder. 'Mary-Lou, I've something to say to you, pet. Do you remember your father at all?'

Startled, Mary-Lou sat upright again. 'Father? No! How could I? I was only three when he went away. I know his photo, of course, but I can't remember a thing about him. Why?'

'I rather thought it would be like that,' said Jo. 'Mary-Lou, you must be very good to Mother when you see her again. Word has come that the Murray-Cameron Expedition has been lost. Only two men have got back – and neither of them is your father.'

'I don't understand quite? What's *really* happened?'

'They met a party of natives who hate white men and

attacked them, and they were all killed except these two who got away. They were right up the Amazon. You do know it's all jungly forest there, don't you? Well, they had an awful time getting back to somewhere where they could tell people, and they only managed to do it a week or two ago. Mother got the news on Monday, and that's why she hasn't been up to see you.'

'Do you – do you mean that – *Father* was killed?' asked Mary-Lou.'

'Just that, darling.' Jo waited, though she scarcely expected that the sad news would affect Mary-Lou very badly. As the child plainly remembered nothing of him, she could hardly grieve much for him. Mary-Lou remained very still, however. Then she suddenly looked up into the tender face above her and said, 'But, Auntie Jo, *why*?'

'Why – what?' asked Jo, rather startled at this reaction.

'Why did they kill them? They weren't doing any harm, were they? Father only went to find new butterflies and insects, and make a c'llection, and things like that. That wouldn't hurt them?'

'No; but I suppose the natives couldn't understand that. They are a very wild tribe, who rarely see anyone but their own people, and they were afraid of the white men. When people are terribly frightened, they sometimes do very cruel things because they *are* so frightened. Perhaps they were afraid that *they* would be killed if they didn't – didn't get in first,' said Jo, resorting to schoolgirl language in a difficulty.

'I see.' Mary-Lou remained silent for a minute or two. Then she asked, 'Does – does Mother mind very much, Auntie Jo?'

'Yes, Mary-Lou. He was her husband, you see, and they loved each other dearly. You can't understand yet, but you will when you're older. And he was Gran's son, so she is very unhappy too, and that's why she's ill. When you see them again, I want you to be very gentle and kind and good to help to comfort them.' Jo paused at that.

Mary-Lou, so precocious in some ways, was a mere baby in others. Would she understand the rest of what was to be said, or should it be left alone? Jo decided to say it. If she did not understand now, she would remember and understand as she grew older, and Jo Maynard had a theory that this was the best way. So she went on: 'You see, pet, you are partly your mother and partly your father. Each of us is that. To Mother and Gran, you are especially your father's own little girl. For that reason you are the one who can comfort them better than anyone else.'

'But please,' said Mary-Lou, 'I'm me – I'm not half anyone.'

Jo sat back and looked at the little round face before her.

'I've seen your father's photo, and you are very like him. Your mouth and nose look like his, and you must be fair like him, for Mother is dark-haired, and hasn't much colour, and her eyes are grey. And your Gran once told me that you were like him in character – I mean, you think the same way as he used to when he was a little boy, and do things as he did. That is because you are his little girl, and so you "take after" him, as people say.'

'Oh, that!' Mary-Lou understood now. 'Gran's often said, "Your father all over again!" when I'd done anything awfully bad. Was that what she meant? I didn't know.'

'Yes; that was what she meant. And because of all this it will help them both if you love them and let them see that you love them by your ways, and the way you speak.'

Mary-Lou looked dismayed. 'I *do* love them – awfully much. But – but do you mean I've got to go kissing them all the time and things like that?' she demanded.

Sad as she felt for all the Trelawneys, Jo nearly burst out laughing at this. She knew that Mary-Lou was as much given to demonstration as any boy, and if the small girl suddenly changed in that way, her family would be startled beyond words. She controlled herself and said. 'No; I don't mean that. It wouldn't be you, and whatever else you are,

112

Mary-Lou, do be *you*. But try to help them, and do as they say without argument – in short, try to be good.'

But Mary-Lou had thought of something else quite suddenly. 'I say! Verity-Ann's father was there too. Is – is he one of the men who got away?'

'Who was he?' asked Jo.

'His name was Mr. Carey, and he did the maps and things.'

Jo looked relieved. 'Then he got away. The other man was Dr. O'Brien, who was making a study of the – the sort of illnesses the natives get, and the causes for them.'

'I'm glad of that,' said Mary-Lou soberly. 'I've got Mother and Gran; but Verity-Ann hasn't anyone else 'cept a solicitor. It would have been *dreadful* for her if he'd been killed. Are they all right?'

'Not quite, dear. They were both hurt, and it's thought that the natives believed them to be dead too, or I'm afraid they would have been killed as well. Luckily, something seems to have startled them, and they fled before they could make sure that all the white men were dead. And Dr. O'Brien, being a doctor, was able to do something for Mr. Carey, and see to his own wounds. But that was one reason why they were so long in getting to safety. And, of course, they had to suffer a good many unpleasant things – being short of food, and so on; so they aren't what you could call well. Is Verity-Ann a great friend of yours?'

Mary-Lou considered. 'Well, we are a *little* more than just acquaintances,' she said carefully. 'I think you might say we were *friendish*. We're not chums like Jo and Vi and Doris and I are. Who's going to tell her – you?'

Jo shook her head. 'No; Miss Annersley will, I expect. But Mother asked me to come and tell you, as she can't leave Gran at the moment. How old is Verity-Ann?'

'About my age – a bit younger, I b'lieve.' Then Mary-Lou added carefully, 'I'm glad *her* father's come back. She'd be so alone if he hadn't. You can't call a s'licitor much home for people, can you?'

'No, indeed! The poor mite!' said Jo, her warm heart at once beginning to revolve ideas for making up, as far as she could, for Verity-Ann's lack of home – at any rate until her father was able to see to her.

Mary-Lou looked at her kind friend wistfully. 'I – I wish *you* could be the one to tell her, Auntie Jo. Miss Annersley's a dear, but you – well, you'd explain it better to her, I think. And Verity-Ann is such a queer kid. Her granny-people that she used to live with were kind to her, but they were awfully *old*.'

'Were they?' said Jo, rather discounting this. To Mary-Lou's age, 'granny-people' would be 'awfully old' whether they were merely in the late fifties or the early nineties.

'Yes; and they expected her always to behave like a little lady,' said Mary-Lou, rather as if this were a terrible hardship. 'I think it's what makes her so queer now.'

'Well, I'll see Miss Annersley before I go and talk it over with her. But as her father's coming back, it isn't quite the same. And he will get all right in time, you know.'

'All right.' Then Mary-Lou suddenly turned red. 'I'm awfully sorry, you know – about Father, I mean – but I don't feel so awfully sad, 'cos I didn't know him – not really him. Do you think it's very horrid of me not to want to cry?'

'No,' said Jo simply. 'It's only natural. To you he is just a photo and someone you've heard about, but nothing more. But don't say anything like that to Mother or Gran, Mary-Lou, because it would hurt them. You see, they *did* know him, and they are very sad indeed, just as you would have been if you had known him. But I don't think it's horrid of you.'

Jo spoke quite gravely, but inwardly she was consumed with wild laughter. Mary-Lou was taking it all in such a matter-of-fact way. She was very glad for the child's sake that it should be so; and more than glad that she had been the one to have to tell the news, and not Mrs. Trelawney.

'I'm glad,' said Mary-Lou, ''cos I don't mean to be horrid.'

114

'Of course you don't! And now, you bad child, kindly tell me what you mean by overworking so much that you've had to be put to bed for a few days. I never heard of such a thing at your age!'

Mary-Lou reddened again. 'I wanted to be moved up,' she said.

'But why? It'll come next September, anyhow. Why this violent hurry? You're in the right form for age, aren't you?'

'Yes; I s'pose so. Most of us are ten or eleven.'

'Well then?'

'I – I didn't want to be so far behind Clem.'

'Oh, I see. But Clem is three or four years older than you, isn't she? Unless you're an infant prodigy – which I'm certain you're *not*, thank goodness! I don't like them – you could scarcely hope to get up to her. Why, when you are thirteen or fourteen, she'll be seventeen or eighteen, and thinking about the University or an Art School, or something like that.'

'Well, it doesn't matter now, 'cos I'll be right down, and there won't be a chance of it,' wailed Mary-Lou.

'For one week's loss of marks? Don't be so silly!' said Jo bracingly, rather thankful to have got off the subject of the Murray-Cameron disaster. 'The thing for you to do is to work hard and steadily all the time you're at lessons, and when it's playtime to put them right out of your head and have a good time. And whatever you do, never try to do them just before you go to sleep. That's simply *asking* for trouble!'

'Oh, Miss Annersley made both me and Clem promise we'd never do such a thing again,' said Mary-Lou with a sigh. 'Auntie Jo, do you really think that if I do as you say I'll get my remove after all?'

'Couldn't tell you. There's a chance, I think, if you go on steadily and don't make a little moke of yourself, trying to overload your brain when you're tired out already.'

'All right. I won't do it again. But I *will* do all I can at lessons. I like them, you know. They're jolly int'resting –

even arith isn't so bad now I know how to do the sums.'

'Good! Steady, honest work is all that's asked of any-one. If I could only be sure that monkey of a Margot did as much, I'd be a thankful woman!'

'No; but Margot is aw-fully clever, you know. I know she doesn't slog like Con and Len; but when she does, she can go right up above them – Len told me so.'

'That's all very well; but sudden fits of slogging, and then resting on your oars for a good while, doesn't get you far. If Margot isn't careful, she'll be left behind when next September comes, and I don't think she'll like that.'

'Have you told her?' asked Mary-Lou.

'Not yet; but I shall. It may make her try to work more steadily. Don't *you* say anything, Mary-Lou,' added Jo in sudden alarm. 'Margot would hate it, and we needn't make it any harder than it is for her to keep her temper.'

'Of course I won't. Oh, Auntie Jo! Are you going already?'

'My dear girl, I've been here nearly an hour. I want to see Hil – Miss Annersley, and I can't stay away much longer. Michael will be wanting me.' Jo bent to kiss the little round face held up to her. 'Good-bye, Mary-Lou. Be a good girl, and get well as fast as you can. I'll pop over again before long to see how you are all getting on. Any message for Mother and Gran? I'm calling there on my way home.'

'Give them my love, please, and say I'm sorry Gran's not well. And – and – tell Mother I'm so sorry about Father. Oh, and I'm heaps better now, and shall most likely go back to school on Monday, Nurse said. And please ask Mother to come and see me as soon as she can. Can you remember all that?'

'I might if I try. Now once more, good-bye, chicken!' Jo gave her a final kiss, and departed.

Eventually there came a tap at the door, and then it opened as Mary-Lou rolled over, and an untidy red-brown head was poked round it.

116

'Clem!' cried Mary-Lou. 'Oh, Clem! How did you get here?'

'It's all right. Matey said I might come for ten minutes at the end of morning school. How are you now?' asked Clem, coming to sit on the foot of the bed with a very friendly look in those red-brown eyes of hers.

'I'm all right, really; but they say I've got to stay here for a day or two. I don't mind; I felt awfully tired, and my head got so swimmy sometimes. It's all right now, though. I say, Clem!'

'Well – what?' demanded Clem as Mary-Lou paused.

'Auntie Jo – Mrs. Maynard, I mean – has just been to see me.'

. 'Jolly decent of her. But then she always seems to be decent. Was your mother or Gran with her, or was she alone?'

'Alone; Gran's very poorly and in bed, and Mother can't leave her, Auntie Jo says. But, Clem, she told me that – that Father won't ever come back from the Amazon.'

'Why ever not?' asked Clem, staring.

' 'Cos he's been killed there,' replied Mary-Lou simply.

Clem was not sure what to say or do. Ought she to try and comfort Mary-Lou – call her fond names, or kiss her, even? But Mary-Lou did not look as if she wanted that. And then the moment passed – much to boyish Clem's relief – and Mary-Lou went on with what was uppermost in her mind.

'I'm awfully sorry, you know, Clem, but – but – well, it isn't the same thing as it would be if it had been *your* father, f'rinstance, that had got killed. You and Tony have known him all your lives, so I s'pose you'd feel you wanted to cry, and be dreadfully miserable. But I can't do that. Is it mean of me?'

Clem considered. 'I don't think so. But you'd better not talk like that to the others. They mightn't understand, and I do. I suppose we *would* feel rather off if Dad died or anything. He's the limit, sometimes; but he's Dad, for

117

all that. But, as you say, we've always had him with us, and you were only a baby when your father went away. I don't see how you could possibly miss him. And I shouldn't think much of you if you pretended just for the looks of the thing,' she added.

'Oh, I couldn't do *that*!' said Mary-Lou, shocked. 'Wouldn't it be acting a lie? Gran always says that while its bad enough to *tell* one, it's ten times worse to *act* one.'

'So it is,' said Clem, who had a sturdy sense of truth of her own. 'I think I'd say as little about it to the others as I could, if I were you.'

'*I* shan't talk about it. I don't feel like it. But I don't know what Verity-Ann will do. Her father was with the same Expedition, but he got away – and the doctor – though he's been hurt.'

'Verity-Ann won't talk,' said Clem with decision. 'She's the rummiest kid I've ever known – and I've known a few in my time. What do you think is her latest?' And Clem settled herself down to give Mary-Lou all the school news she could in the time, thankful that the need for being 'comforting' had passed.

So it was left there. On the following Monday, Mary-Lou rejoined her form, completely restored to herself, and having learned thoroughly a lesson against overdoing at her work. No one except Clem and Verity-Ann knew of the big change that had come into her life. For it *was* a big change, as Mary-Lou realized more and more as time went on. Mother always looked very sad, though she roused herself when her little girl was with her, and Gran seemed to have become a very old lady all at once. Mary-Lou felt dimly that things would never be quite the same again, now that they couldn't look forward any more to Father coming home. Mercifully, as the grown-ups knew, she was too small to know it altogether, and she would grow up with the idea of it.

As Jo Maynard said to the younger Mrs. Trelawney once when they were talking together, 'No one wants babies of her age to have their lives shadowed at the beginning. It's bad for you and Mrs. Trelawney, I know; but at least you can be glad of the fact that Mary-Lou hasn't to know a *bitter* sorrow. And I know what I'm saying. When my little girls were only three, I thought for several awful days that Jack had been drowned at sea. Even then, I was grateful for the fact that the children would not be saddened by his loss as they must have been if he had been a part of their daily lives as he is now, for instance.'

And Mother, with a sudden feeling of thankfulness that this was so, fully agreed with her.

CHAPTER ELEVEN

MARY-LOU GOES HOME

'GOOD-BYE, Mary-Lou. Will you please tell your mother, if you think she would like to hear from me, that I'm so sorry it was *my* father and a stranger who escaped from the natives. I do so wish it had been my father and yours. But as it is, it can't be helped now. But I should have been so glad if it had been your father, too.' Verity-Ann finished her speech with an elderly sigh.

Mary-Lou, who had been staring at her in amazement, began to laugh. 'Oh, Verity-Ann! You *did* s'prise me just at first! I thought you were going to say you were sorry your father had escaped anyhow.'

Verity-Ann's small face flushed. 'I could never say that, Mary-Lou. You ought to know that. He is my father, even if I don't know him, and it would be very wicked of me to wish such a thing about my own father. I don't, of course. I – I'm very glad he escaped.' Then she added with the sudden frankness which the others were beginning to expect from her. 'But I'm not really *excitingly* glad about it. Perhaps I'm bad after all.'

Mary-Lou looked at her thoughtfully as she pulled on her gloves. 'No; I don't think you are,' she said slowly. 'Auntie Jo would say that it was just natural. I know what you mean. You feel like me – only the other way round – when I can't be horribly miserable because my father died. Auntie Jo said I'd never really known him, so it couldn't be done. But I must remember that Mother and Gran had – known him, I mean – that they were very sad. So, you see, I'm sorry for them, so I'm sorry in a way. And you can be glad for – for — ' She came to a full stop as she suddenly remembered that Verity-Ann had no one to be glad for.

That little person turned great blue eyes on her. 'Yes; but you see I haven't any mother or grandmother, so I have no one to be glad for but myself,' she said, not at all sadly, but just stating the fact.

'Well, you can be glad for that,' said Mary-Lou. 'He's your father, anyhow. He b'longs to you, and if he hadn't come back, there'd have been no one. You think of that, and I expect you'll soon be really *very* glad.'

'I might try. Yes, Mary-Lou; you are quite right. I might have been like Jacynth Hardy, who hasn't anyone really hers. But I shall have Father now. Thank you; that is a help.'

'There's Auntie Jo and the car!' cried Mary-Lou, ignoring this. 'Hoo-ooo, Auntie Jo! I'm here, and the Trips are coming soon.'

'And the *who*?' demanded Jo Maynard as she stopped the car and got out. '*What* was that you said, Mary-Lou?'

Mary-Lou went red. 'It – it – well, that's what everyone calls them here, Auntie Jo.'

'Oh, indeed! Well, I might have guessed it.' Jo spoke with resignation. 'Just the same, Mary-Lou, I'd rather you didn't to me at any rate. Well, Verity-Ann, ought you to be out here in the cold with only your blazer, dear?' Then she bent down to kiss the little fair face with motherly tenderness. Jo Maynard was desperately sorry for Verity-Ann, but that small lady was very reserved,

120

and she was unaccustomed to the petting which Jo's own family looked on as part of their daily life, and rather shrank away from it. Only to Mary-Lou, with whom she had a funny, rather one-sided friendship, could she open out to any extent. Jo noticed it, and felt even sorrier. It told her so much about Verity-Ann's home-life.

'Next term you must come and spend a Saturday at Plas Gwyn with my girls and Mary-Lou,' she said, releasing the child. 'Now, where *are* those girls of mine? Run and see, Mary-Lou. I want to get home.'

'Mamma – Mamma!' Len suddenly appeared and flung herself on her mother. 'Matey wouldn't let us come before, 'cos my drawer was in a mess, and Con's shoe-lace got into a knot and Matey wouldn't let her cut it. And Margot never stripped her bed prop'ly this morning, so Matey's scolded her like anything. So we're *all* late. Con's coming now, and so's Margot when she's washed. Matey made her *howl*!'

'I'll bet she did!' Jo spoke with some feeling. In her own schooldays she had had to endure many a sharp reproof herself from Matey, and she could well imagine that her youngest daughter had wept over what had been said to her.

However, the missing pair came racing up at that moment, so she bundled Mary-Lou, Len and Con into the back seat of the car, and popped Margot into the front beside her, wisely saying nothing about the rather red eyes under the golden curls.

'Run along in out of the wind, Verity-Ann,' she advised. 'You'll catch cold if you stand here in this wind.' Then she got in, slammed the door shut, and the next moment they were off, the four small girls waving wildly to Verity-Ann, who responded gravely before she ran into the house, there to be caught by Matron, who exclaimed in horror at her icy hands, and sent her to the common-room to warm herself properly, with orders not to do such a stupid thing again.

'Where's young Clem?' asked Jo of Mary-Lou. She

felt a fondness for blunt, honest Clem, whom she had already met two or three times.

'Gone to Armiford to spend the day with her godfather – lucky wretch,' replied Mary-Lou. 'Miss Burnett took her 'cos Miss Linton's had to go to Exeter to her sister as her baby's ill – the sister's, I mean.'

'I'm sorry to hear that.' Jo sounded concerned; she felt it, too. Joyce Linton, now Joyce Erroll, was disposed to make large demands on her sister, who, though little more than a year older than herself, had mothered the younger girl ever since their own mother had shown signs of the illness that eventually carried her off.

Joyce had been a byword at school for selfishness and egotism; and though her years there had greatly improved her, there were times when the old Joyce popped up, and she was disposed to think that her sister must give her first attention, whatever else went.

'How is Mike?' asked Len as they turned out of the avenue.

'Splendid – the biggest of you all. He's getting huge now.'

'I saw Katharine Lucy last week,' put in Mary-Lou.

Jo began to laugh. 'Are they really calling her by her full name?'

'I 'spect so. Why, Auntie Jo?'

'Because they've never yet succeeded in calling any one of their crowd by their full names – except John. She'll be "Kitty" or "Kate" before many more weeks pass. What is she like, Mary-Lou?'

'Just ducky! I never saw a baby as wee as that. Mike wasn't so very tiny when I saw him first.'

'Mamma, when can *we* see her?' Con demanded.

'Not till the hols, my lamb. Then we'll ask the whole family to come for a week-end, as there'll be only ourselves at home then – except for Auntie Rob.'

'If there's snow, can we go sledgin'?'

'You three and Steve may. You won't hurt in the

meadow – and that's where you'll do most of your sledging unless Papa or I are with you.'

'Auntie Jo, how are Mother and Gran?' Mary-Lou asked suddenly.

'Your mother is being very plucky. Your Gran is only poorly, though. Help them all you can, Mary-Lou.' Jo spoke soberly.

'Oh, I mean to – truly I do.' Then Mary-Lou added, 'D'you know, Auntie, I rather think Verity-Ann's *afraid* of her father. You see, she hasn't seen him for such ages.'

'That won't do!' Jo spoke emphatically. 'I must try to have a talk with her. Are you sure, Mary-Lou?'

'She hasn't really said so, but I sort of feel she is. I hoped you'd do something, Auntie. She's – she's so *queer*!"' Mary-Lou ended up helplessly.

'I'll talk to her, my lamb. Don't worry about it. We'll try to prevent Verity-Ann from hurting her father's feelings if we can.'

Mary-Lou heaved a sigh of relief. 'That's what I meant. Thanks awfully, Auntie Jo.'

'Here's Carn Beg!' cried Len. 'And there's Auntie Doris at the door. May we go and kiss her Mamma?'

'Just one kiss, then. You mustn't stay for anything more,' said Jo, opening the doors for them.

They all tumbled out, and headed by Mary-Lou, raced up the long path to the door where Mrs. Trelawney stood waiting. Mary-Lou was hugged first. Then the Triplets had their turn.

'Mamma's calling!' Len said as she lifted her face for a second kiss. 'We must go. Good-bye, Auntie Doris! We all love you heaps.'

'Come *on*, you three!' shouted Jo from the car. 'Doris, I'll see you some time sooner or later.' She bundled her trio back into the car, and they drove off.

Mrs. Trelawney, an arm round Mary-Lou's shoulders, pulled her into the house and shut the door against the cold wind.

In the drawing-room, where a glorious log fire was

blazing, she sat down and drew her little girl before her, looking at the small round face with hungry eyes.

'Aren't I clean?' Mary-Lou asked, beginning to wriggle.

'Quite clean, dear. I only wanted to be sure that you were no worse for overworking as you did. You mustn't do that again.'

'No; I know. Everyone's gone on at Clem and me like fun about it,' admitted Mary-Lou. She perched herself on the arm of Mother's chair, put an arm round her neck, and gave her a quick hug. 'Mother, if ever there's anything I can do to help you, you'll let me, won't you?'

'Yes, darling. And you *do* help, just by being Father's little girl.'

Mrs. Trelawney spoke hurriedly and with a catch in her voice.

Mary-Lou was horrified. Grown-ups never did cry, but Mother sounded horribly like it. 'How – how is Gran?' she asked quickly.

'She hasn't been very well for some days. Go and hang your things up, dear, and then you shall come and see her for a few minutes.'

They went upstairs arm-in-arm – a new departure. Once it would have been hand-in-hand, but Mary-Lou had shed the last of her baby ways. Gran was sitting by the fire in her bedroom, wrapped in shawls. She looked frail and old somehow; but when she spoke, it was Gran herself.

'Well, so here you are at last! That's what comes of having no sense. I hope you've behaved yourself lately?'

Mary-Lou kissed her. 'I think so. I've only had a row or two for spilling ink and things like that – nothing to count.'

'Thank goodness you'll learn to be tidy at school,' said Gran.

'How are you, Gran?'

'Much better, thank you. Quite well again by Christmas, I hope. Stand over there and let me look at you.'

Mary-Lou obeyed, outwardly meek, but inwardly wishing that people *wouldn't* want to stare. It made her feel so silly.

Gran looked her over. 'You've grown *again*!' she said accusingly. 'Just look at your frock! It's little more than a frill round your waist – almost indecent I call it!'

Mary-Lou bent to look at the hem of her brief skirt. 'Matey said I'd have to have it let down in the hols,' she admitted. 'All my other frocks too. But I can't help growing, Gran. I just do it.'

'Oh, I'm not sorry. None of our family have even been small and I've no use for shrimps. Your hair's growing too, I'm glad to see. In another year's time it should be getting near your waist.'

'It's an awful bore,' her grand-daughter told her. 'Clem has to plait for me in the mornings. I can't do it myself – not yet.'

'Ah! The redoubtable Clem! Well, I suppose you know you are to have her and her imp of a brother here for Christmas?'

'Oh, has Mrs. Barras written then?' Mary-Lou demanded eagerly.

'Yes – a very proper letter, for a wonder! She also sent your mother a cheque to buy presents for them, as she says there's nothing in that outlandish place where they are. See if you can find out what they would like. I believe in giving people what they want.'

'Right! I will,' Mary-Lou promised happily. She came to sit on the hassock at Gran's feet. 'It'll be jolly fun having them. We can all play with the Maynards, and I expect the Russells'll be coming too. Clem and Sybil Russell are quite pally. If only it's fine we can be out, and then we can yell as much as we like without bothering you.'

'So school hasn't sobered either you or Miss Clem down? How does she get on, by the way?'

'Oh, awfully well. She's got lots of friends in her own form – Sybil and the Lucy girls, and Bride Bettany, and some others. But here's a weird thing, Gran. I'm three years younger'n her, and we're chums still. The first day

125

or two I wondered if it would make a difference, me being so much younger and two forms lower. But it hasn't. It might have, though.'

'Your Clem is loyal,' said Gran. 'That's a good point in her character. And what about you? You've plenty of other friends too?'

'Yes – oh, yes! But Clem is different. And,' Mary-Lou added slowly, 'even though we've both got heaps of other friends, it only seems to make us – well – *better* pals.'

'If school has taught you that, Mary-Lou,' said Gran, looking gravely into the blue eyes, 'it has taught you something that will help you all your life.'

'I don't think I understand.'

Gran considered. 'What I mean is this. Learn to share your friends with other people. If they're friends worth having, and if *you* are a friend worth having, they and you will be all the closer for it. It's the people who demand everything and won't share who are to be doubted. Never be jealous or exacting or selfish in your friendships. And never give in to that sort of thing either, or you'll only end by making yourself and the other person miserable.'

She leaned back in her chair, looking suddenly tired, and Mother saw this, even while Mary-Lou was frowning with the effort to impress Gran's words on her memory.

'You're looking tired, Madre. Mary-Lou and I will go downstairs and have our cocoa while you rest. She's going to Plas Gwyn for the afternoon, but when she comes back she shall come to sit with you a while before she goes to bed. Let me tuck you up.' And she set to work to make Gran comfortable, while Mary-Lou, looking on, realized that Gran really *was* an old lady, and also how much the loss of Father must mean to her and Mother. She was glad to be hurried downstairs, where she and Mother had cocoa and biscuits in the drawing-room, and where Mother, noticing her sudden silence, asked a leading question about school, which soon brought back the chatter in full spate.

Mary-Lou told Mother everything about school and her

chums – especially Clem, and when lunch-time came, what Mrs. Trelawney didn't know about it all wasn't worth knowing!

After lunch, Mary-Lou was told to wrap up and run round to Plas Gwyn.

'By the road, mind, Mary-Lou. You'd get your feet soaked if you tried to cross the meadow. You're going to church with the Maynards tomorrow morning, as I can't leave Gran; but in the afternoon we'll be together.'

Mary-Lou nodded. 'That'll be wizard!' She slipped her arm round Mother's waist as they stood together, and looked up into her face. 'Mother, Gran isn't really awfully ill, is she?'

'She's not very well, dear.' Mother paused a moment. Then she went on: 'Mary-Lou, we don't expect you to feel sad about Father. You never really knew him, for you were only a baby when he went away. But as you grow older, you will be very proud of him, I think. I had a letter from Commander Carey – Verity-Ann's father – and he told me that Father could have escaped when the natives set on the camp. He wasn't with them at the time, and was just coming back when he saw what was happening. If he had turned round and crept away he might have got off safely. But he wouldn't desert his friends without trying to do something to help them. So he rushed in to the fight, and Commander Carey saw one of the natives kill him.'

Mary-Lou suddenly buried her face against Mother, and her grip round the slender waist tightened. 'That was – that was —' she began in muffled tones. Then she changed her sentence. 'But, Mother, he was a hero, then! He was killed because he went to help them.'

Mother looked down into the glowing blue eyes Mary-Lou raised to hers. 'Yes, dear. But that is the sort of thing real friendship means.'

And then she quoted softly: ' "Greater love hath no man than this, that a man lay down his life for his friends." I don't want you to feel sad, Mary-Lou; but I do want you to grow up being proud of Father. And I want you to feel that you must be brave and loyal and true as he was. You must never do anything to disgrace his record of courage and truth and loyalty?'

'No,' said Mary-Lou gravely. She hoped Mother would say no more at present, for her small head was whirling. Father had been a hero, like a history person! She wanted to get away somewhere and think about it.

Luckily, having said so much, Mother only bent to kiss her, and then sent her off to Plas Gwyn.

It was great fun to be in the nursery there and to play with 'La Maison des Poupées' as the big dolls' house was grandly called.

After tea, Mary-Lou was given the treat of helping to put Michael to bed, while the Triplets cleared the nursery. Then the small girl was able to talk a little of the great news which had filled her mind all the time, even when they were playing their hardest.

'Did you know about Father being a hero, Auntie Jo?' she asked as she brought the warm towels.

Jo looked at her, her black eyes full of a soft fire. 'Yes, I know. I called at Carn Beg yesterday, and your mother told me. And knowing it is going to help her and your Gran to live without the hope of having him home again one day. I hope it will help *you* to grow up into the sort of girl who ought to have a hero for a father.'

'How?'

'By being straight, and truthful; never hiding anything, or saying something that makes other people think one thing when really you mean another. You've got to try your hardest always – for goodness' sake, Mary-Lou, don't turn into a spiv or a slacker! There's nothing sloppier or more despicable in this world, I think.'

'I loathe sloppy things!' Mary-Lou told her with fervour.

'I should hope so. Bring me the soap and sponge now. When he's in, you can help to sponge him. You aren't likely to wet yourself in that overall. Another thing, Mary-Lou,' went on Jo as she slipped off the last of Michael's tiny garments, and let him lie kicking and gurgling on her

128

lap, 'you must be a *good* friend, for he was one. He gave his life to help his friends. Friendship means all that. And it means being kind, and trying not to hurt other people's feelings, even when they make you feel angry or impatient with them. Lots of folk would be horrified if they knew how much they hurt others by unkind words or actions. Lots of times others' funny little ways and words may irritate you almost beyond bearing. But for goodness' sake try to hold your horses, and keep your tongue quiet. You've probably just as many trying habits. Learn to make allowances for others.'

'Right-ho!' Mary-Lou jumped up from the low stool on which she had been sitting, for Anna came in with the big cans of hot and cold water, and when Auntie Jo had tested the temperature of the mixture with her elbow, Michael was popped in. He sat shrieking delightedly, and splashing vigorously. Jo soaped him carefully, and then let the small girl squeeze the sponge over him until all the soap was gone, and he was lifted out on to the warm towel and dry-patted.

'Now you can go to the others, Mary-Lou,' said his mother as she picked up the big puff. 'I'll bring him along to say good-night when he's ready. Hop off – scoot – vamoose – scram!'

Mary-Lou chuckled and danced off to join in a riotous game of 'Statues' with the Triplets, which lasted till Jo appeared in the doorway between the two nurseries, a sleepy and contented Michael in her arms, and they all crowded round to kiss him good night. Then Anna took her home, and the evening ended with another talk with Mother.

'Mother!' Mary-Lou turned on the settee where they were sitting to face Mother. 'I want to ask you something.'

'What is it, dear?'

'Will you tell me all about Father, please? You see, I never really knew him. I was just a kid when he went away. I'd like to know more about him. Will you, Mother?'

For a moment Doris Trelawney caught her breath. Then

she lifted her head proudly. Whatever it cost, Father's child must know him as well as possible. 'Yes, dear; I'll tell you all I can,' she said quietly.

'Could you – could you begin – now?' asked Mary-Lou hesitatingly.

'Yes, dear; the sooner the better.'

So they sat cuddled up together on the big settee in the dancing firelight, and Mother began to tell her 'all about Father'. It was a long story, and when the holidays came, was carried on for half an hour every night; for Clem and Tony were eager to hear too.

As Clem said, 'I'd like to know as much as I can about such a splendid man, Mrs. Trelawney. So if you don't mind Tony and me listening we'd like to, please. If you'd rather just have Mary-Lou alone, we can go to bed. Honest, we shouldn't mind!'

But by that time Mother was ready to tell the story to honest, enthusiastic Clem; and Tony, with his sensitive feeling for other people, should also know how one Englishman had grown up, so that when the hour of testing came he, too, might not be found wanting.

But on this night it was Mary-Lou alone who heard how Mother had first met Father more than twelve years before. When the story ended, it was long past nine o'clock, and Mother looked horrified when she saw the clock. Mary-Lou was chased off to bed forthwith, with orders to get to sleep as quickly as she could. But when Mother came up half an hour later she was still awake. Mother stooped over her to give her a good-night kiss, and Mary-Lou flung her arms round her in a quick, fierce hug while she whispered, 'I'll try, Mother – honest, I will!'

And Mother, returning the hug, understood all she meant to say.

CHAPTER TWELVE

A SINGING LESSON

THE rest of the week-end seemed to go like a flash. Mary-Lou sadly realized this as she climbed the stairs to go to bed on Sunday night at eight o'clock. The next morning she got up to begin the day that was soon to become known in the annals of the school as 'the day of that awful music row'.

Auntie Jo arrived with the car dead on time, and Mary-Lou grabbed her satchel, kissed Mother good-bye and scrambled into the coveted front seat, which had been left for her, and away they whirled to school, where an excited Clem was looking out for her, and grabbed her promptly.

'Here you are at last! I thought you were never coming! Oh, Mary-Lou, I had a letter from Mums this morning, and she says your mother has asked Tony and me for the hols! How absolutely wizard of her! Did you know about it?'

'Rather! Mother told me ages ago she was writing to Mrs. Barras to ask if you might. It was about the first thing she told me when I got home on Friday – that your mother had said you could.'

'Well, I think she's a perfect pet to have thought of it. I — ' Clem paused. Then she went on quickly, 'I don't say anything about it, for it's no use howling over spilt milk, but I *was* feeling frightfully sick about not seeing Tony till Easter – and not then, perhaps. But it's all right now.'

'I'm glad to hear that. whatever it is,' said a voice behind them, and they swung round to find Gay Lambert standing looking at them as severely as she could. 'Other things, I might mention, are all wrong. This happens to be French day, and you ought not to be speaking in English –

131

neither should I,' she added, changing with stunning suddenness to French, so that they both gasped audibly. 'Besides that, you are in the corridor, so you ought not to be talking *at all*! You can each lose a conduct mark. And you, Mary-Lou, had better cut off and change, or you'll be late for Prayers.'

Mary-Lou glanced at the clock at the end of the corridor, gave vent to another gasp, and scuttled off as fast as she could go. It was a breathless scrimmage, but she contrived to enter the form-room just two seconds ahead of Miss Carey, who was taking duty for Miss Linton.

Work at the Chalet School was always strenuous during lesson periods, and Miss Carey, taking over as much as she could of Miss Linton's work, was not so sweet-tempered as usual, so they dared not whisper or play. To make matters worse, as the morning went on, a fine rain began to fall, and this was the day when Upper Second A had their games. No one would allow them to go out in rain like that, so it meant they must play handball in the Gym, which would not be nearly so much fun. Altogether, it was a badly disgruntled mob of little girls who swarmed to the Splasheries after lessons to wash their hands and tidy their hair. As it was 'French' day, they were unable to express themselves as freely as they would have liked, but they did their best, even Verity-Ann producing a severe 'Je n'aime pas la pluie!' to Mary-Lou, who happened to be sharing a basin with her.

'Moi aussi,' said Mary-Lou gloomily. She had been looking forward to netball, for she was making steady progress now, and loved the game.

There was no time for more. Miss Carey had not been satisfied with their history, and had kept them after the bell went, so that the gong sounded while a good many people were still struggling with untidy heads, or wrangling about the towels. They had to hurry to their places in the long procession, however, and as Mary-Lou sat at one table between Sybil Russell and a Fifth Former, she had to content herself with scowling fiercely during the meal.

Things were made worse for her by a remark from Mollie Avery, also at the table, which informed her that something had gone wrong with the outside heating, so they would not be able to use the Gym.

'It's just too bad!' groused Mary-Lou to herself as she worked her way through a plateful of bread-and-butter pudding. 'That's the last spoonful, thank goodness! I hate this pudding – soppy mess!'

After their half-hour's rest, when she read *Nat the Naturalist* stolidly without taking much of the story in, she and the others gathered in their form-room, and, rules or no rules, gave vent to their grievance in good English – or colloquial English might be more truthful, since they all employed a good deal of slang.

Suddenly the door was flung open, and Vi Lucy burst in, her eyes shining, her face flushed. Josette Russell and Doris Hill followed her, all wildly excited, and Josette raced up to the small platform on which stood the mistress's desk, and thumped on the desk for attention.

'What do you think?' she gabbled when had got it. 'Mlle Berné met us three in the corridor just now, and she said to tell you all that as the weather's so awful, we're to have a special carol prac this afternoon and begin on the quite new carols.'

'Plato's coming for it,' added Doris. 'It's to go on for an hour, and then we have prep till four, and after tea we can have games in here, only we've got to leave the room tidy at supper-time.'

'You're all to get your pencils and carol-books, and be ready to go along to Hall the minute the bell rings!' Vi added her quota, as she hunted madly through a locker which looked as if someone had given it a good stirring-up with a hay-fork.

A buzz of excited exclamations sounded round the room.

'How wizard!' – 'Good egg!' '– Jolly idea!' were capped by a 'Magnifique! Mas tr-r-rès magnifique!' from Mary-Lou in so exactly the tones and manner of Mlle Berné herself, that the rest broke into wild giggles.

'Oh,' went on Josette, 'and we can talk English for the rest of the afternoon – Plato will, you know,' she added.

'I'd like to know why we call Plato "Plato",' said Doris suddenly.

'Oh *I* can tell you that,' said Josette importantly. 'We began almost when the school did – when it was in Tirol and Mummy was Head – and the first lesson he gave, he talked an awful lot of rot about Plato.'

'Who's he?' someone demanded.

'Oh, some Greek or other – I don't really know. But he wrote a lot about music – I do know *that*! Well, Auntie Jo was a Middle then, and *she* called him Plato, and we all have ever since.'

'It's a funny name, isn't it?' Mary-Lou went off into one of her enchanting peals of laughter. 'You know, Jo, I don't think Auntie Jo can have been exactly a *good* little girl!'

'Of course she wasn't!' Josette cried indignantly. 'She wouldn't *dream* of it! "A good little girl!" *O-ow!* It sounds just horrid! Auntie Jo wasn't in the least like that! Mummy once told me she got into the most awful rows sometimes, and kept them all wondering what she would do next. She wasn't in the *least* good – not good *at all*!' This last rather as if being 'good' were something no decent schoolgirl would ever descend to!

'I know,' put in Doris. 'My Auntie Kath used to teach at the school then – she was Miss Leslie, but she went to India when she married Uncle Michael. When I was quite a small kid and she used to stay with us in the hols, she used to tell of the awful things Mrs. Maynard did. But she said she generally *meant* all right, only they didn't turn out as she'd thought they would – like when she ran away to find Princess Elisaveta – the Crown Princess of Belsornia, you know, who'd been kidnapped.'

An excited chorus demanded to know the story, but the bell rang for afternoon school just then, and Miss Carey appeared, and they had to go to their seats for afternoon register before she marshalled them into line, and then

134

marched them off to Hall, where they took their usual places. The rest of the school was either already there, or came in during the next five minutes or so. Miss Cochrane, head of the music staff, was at the piano, and when they were all settled, Plato, or, to give him his correct name, Mr. Denny, marched on to the platform.

Miss Burnett, the history mistress, and one-time head-girl of the school, followed him, and took her seat behind him on the dais.

The girls stood up when the two came in, and he smiled genially at them. 'Good day, young damsels,' he said in the quaint Elizabethan English he generally employed. 'To-day we intend to make acquaintance with some of the carols you are to sing in our new Christmas concert. Attention! Here are some of the airs on these sheets' – he waved a formidable bundle of MS. sheets at them. 'We will distribute them, and see how you manage to read the airs. We will begin with the first, and take it three times before Miss Cochrane is kind enough to play it for us.' He bowed in that lady's direction.

Gillian Culver came forward quickly, and took the bundle, which she divided among the rest of the prefects, and in a few moments the rest of the school were passing them along the lines till every girl had a sheet. The notes were printed on them in his own beautifully clear manuscript, and the girls glanced over the titles on the front with interest, though they dared not turn them to see what was on the other side. They were supposed to be making the most of their time and getting some idea of the first air.

This was an Irish carol, 'Christmas Day is come.' When he considered that they had sufficient time to learn something of what he was wont to call 'the curves of the music', Plato rapped on the desk with his baton, Miss Cochrane struck the chord, and the school rose and did its best to read it at sight. As it was not a difficult air, they managed fairly well. All the elder girls were accustomed to such work, and small people like Verity-Ann and Mary-Lou

135

followed the Seniors as well as they could. They went through it three times. Then the school sat down while Miss Cochrane played it through with the harmonies, and then they rose again and sang it to her accompaniment, 'lah-ing' it, as none of them knew the words. It was highly successful, though there would be a great deal to do in the way of polishing it before Plato was even moderately satisfied – he had been known before this to stop a performance at a concert and turn the concert into a lesson if things did not suit him!

The next one happened to be a Bach carol, 'O, Jesulein süss, O Jesulein mild.' Verity-Ann saw the German title, and her small jaw was instantly squared. Not even after nearly a term at the school had anyone succeeded in reconciling her to the language, and she sat throughout the first efforts at reading it with her lips firmly closed. That was excusable in a first attempt. But when they had read it again, and mastered some of its difficulties, it was to be expected that she would join in.

Now, Verity-Ann had a sweet little voice, very true and clear, and with a lark-like lilt in it that was rare. Plato had found this out during the first lesson he had given Upper Second that term, and he found time in the midst of his conducting to glance across at the demure little maiden, who was rather a favourite with him. As it happened, he knew nothing about Verity-Ann's views on German, never having had any reason to meet them before; and none of the rest of the Staff had told him. So now he was amazed to see her standing there, lips pinched together, obviously making no effort to sing. This was not like her, for as much as she hated German, so much did Verity-Ann love music, and she generally sang with all her might and main. He waited till the carol ended, and then leaned forward and beckoned to her to come to him. Verity-Ann went scarlet to the roots of her silky curls, but she obeyed his finger, and went to stand at the foot of the dais, looking up at him with fearless eyes of gentian-blue.

'You do not sing, little maid,' said Plato mildly.

136

No answer! Verity-Ann did not really know what to say, for one thing. For another, Miss Burnett's eye was on her. She went redder than ever, and remained silent. Plato looked surprised. Of all children, he would not have expected bad manners from Verity-Ann. He bent down to her. 'I spoke to you, little one,' he reminded her gently. 'That demands an answer from you. You do not sing. Not once have you opened your lips, and I missed your little bird-like pipe among the others. What is the reason?'

Thus faced with a direct question. Verity-Ann knew that she must reply. Reply she did. 'I dislike German, and do not approve of either speaking or singing it,' she told him primly.

The astounded man gaped at her for a moment. Then: 'I have not yet asked you to sing the words,' he said slowly.

'The music is by a German. I do not approve of *any* Germans,' she informed him, her eyes lit by a sudden spark.

A splutter – suppressed, it is true, but a splutter all the same – came from the Upper Second row. Miss Burnett removed her eyes from Verity-Ann's small face, and fixed them with an awful glare on Lesley Malcolm and the Carter twins who were sitting together, and who went as red as Verity-Ann had been a moment or two before. They squirmed, and tried to look as if they weren't there, and, satisfied for the time being, Miss Burnett gave her attention to the scene between Verity-Ann and Plato, neither of whom had paid any attention to the interruption. They were too much in earnest over their own particular affair.

'Bach was one of the greatest geniuses this world has ever known,' said the master gravely to Verity-Ann. 'Genius, my little maid, knows no bonds of nationality. It is extra-territorial. For example, our own Shakespeare was English by birth; but his plays are for all the world, as they are for all time. So with music – with all the arts. Now you will go back to your place and sing with the rest as an obedient child should.' He waved her back to her place,

137

and Verity-Ann returned, her face once more crimson.

'Chantez, vous chèvre!' whispered Mary-Lou to her as she pulled her down beside her.

Verity-Ann said nothing, but she drew her arm away from Mary-Lou's grasp. When they stood up to sing again, she opened her mouth, it is true, but no sound came from it. Mary-Lou glanced apprehensively at Plato, who was beginning to frown. If Verity-Ann thought she could get away with anything of that kind, she was badly mistaken. Quite a number of people might have done so, but not the owner of a voice like hers. Those silvery notes had been marked by him, and already he was evolving plans for training them very carefully – in class for the present, with hopes of special lessons later on; and his ear was far too fine to overlook their absence, even when the whole school was singing. He had had the training of a good many of the Chalet School girls, notably Jo Maynard, whose voice, with its golden, chorister-like tones, was unique. In Verity-Ann he fancied he had found an equally unique voice, and one which should, in later years, attain to a power denied to Jo's – a power that might take her to the concert halls in time.

The carol drew to a close, and once it was over, Plato threw down his baton with an angry 'Sit down, all! You, child – Verity-Ann – come here to me!'

No mistaking whom he meant, even if he had not said the name. Once more scarlet, Verity-Ann squeezed past the others, and went to the dais once more.

'Up here – beside me on the dais!' he ordered, his eyes beginning to glow in a way that told the experienced that his temper was beginning to get the better of him.

Verity-Ann went round the front to the steps at the side, and crossed the dais in her usual composed little way, and stood beside him. He looked down on her golden head, which came to just above his elbow, and his lips suddenly twitched with the humour of it. But he must have obedience, so he steadied them.

'You will sing this carol by yourself,' he said firmly.

'Give her the note, please, Miss Cochrane. Thank you! Now begin, child!'

Miss Cochrane, having sounded the first note on the piano, turned to try to frown Verity-Ann into obedience; but that small person paid no heed to her or anyone else. Standing there beside the tall, gaunt Plato, whose sense of humour was beginning to fail him again, and who was looking thoroughly angry, she set her lips and stood gazing out across the heads of the assembled school, obstinately mute.

Miss Burnett felt it was time that she took a hand. She rose from her seat and came forward. 'Verity-Ann, do as you are told,' she said very quietly, but with something in her voice to which most girls knuckled under at once.

Not Verity-Ann! She looked up at Miss Burnett, but said and did nothing more.

Plato lost his temper completely. With a glare that would have reduced most of his pupils to terrified obedience at once, he thundered at her, 'Do as I bid you, Miss; or there is a rod in pickle for you, and one you will not like! Sing at once if you are not ill.'

Verity-Ann turned from Miss Burnett to him. 'I am not ill,' she told him, her clear, silvery tones reaching to the farthest corner of the room. 'I refuse to sing a carol, or a song, or anything by any German, however famous or no-no-tor-ious he may be.'

And from that stand neither the infuriated Plato, nor Miss Burnett, nor even Miss Cochrane's sharp tongue, could move her. She was prepared to sing carols by composers of every other nation under the sun, but sing *German* carols she would not. Finally, Miss Burnett, laid a hand on her shoulder.

'Listen to me, Verity-Ann,' she said. 'You will either do as Mr. Denny tells you at once and without further fuss, or you will go to bed for the rest of the day. Choose, and choose quickly. We cannot have the lesson spoilt for everyone else by your naughtiness and selfishness. Be quick! Bed – or sing; which is it?'

Verity-Ann started a little. She loved singing, though she would sing nothing German. Of all the Upper Second, perhaps, she had most looked forward to the after-tea games, for they had planned that the next time they could, they would have 'dress-up' charades, and that was a game she enjoyed with her whole being. Josette and Vi had already gone to Miss Slater by Miss Carey's kind permission and asked if they might have clothes from the acting cupboards, and Miss Slater had laughed and said yes; only they must bring everything back by seven, neatly folded and in good order. Now she must either do as she was told – of which she had no intention – or she must lose all this joy. If Miss Burnett had devoted a whole week to thinking about it she could have found no punishment that would hit the small girl harder. But – if she wanted her fun, then she must give in, and she had once vowed that she would never, never have anything to do with German if she could help it. Verity-Ann's small pointed jaw was set as firmly as such a jaw could be. She would *not* give in!

Miss Burnett saw it. With that firm hand on the little shoulder, she turned to Plato with an apology, and then steered the small girl to the door. She took her out, shutting the door behind them, and the angry Plato turned to the rest with a curt command to take up their sheets and sing the carol over again. They did as they were told with a promptness that should have gladdened his heart, but all the delight had gone from the lesson. Plato was furious at being defied thus by Miss Four-foot-nothing, and Miss Cochrane of the peppery temper was even more so. That much was plain to all from the way in which she pounded out the airs of the piano. Miss Burnett came back, having handed over Verity-Ann to the tender mercies of Matron, and Lesley and the twins shook in their shoes at her expression. She said nothing to them, however, until the lesson ended, and Plato, a very black frown on his brow, had stalked out of Hall. Then Nemesis fell.

'Stand, all of you!' said Miss Burnett incisively. 'The three little girls who behaved so badly will stay behind;

the rest will march to their form-rooms and begin their preparation at once. Thank you, Miss Cochrane.'

Miss Cochrane struck up a march, and the school marched out, leaving the three sinners very sorry for themselves. They were sorrier still before Miss Cochrane had done with them. She told them exactly what she thought of their manners and did it in her most unpleasant voice. The twins were weeping, and Lesley on the verge of tears. Finally, she condemned them all to writing apologies to the singing master, to spending their precious evening time in hemming dusters for Matron in their form-room, and to losing two conduct marks each. She sent them off to their preparation after that in no state to produce any good work, so there were repercussions later on when dissatisfied mistresses wanted to know what they had been doing!

All in all, it was a most unpleasant singing lesson, and Verity-Ann was not allowed to forget it in a hurry, either. Her own punishment was unpleasant enough. She not only had to apologize to Plato for her bad behaviour – and she was a proud little mortal, and hated saying she was sorry to anyone – she was also told that since she would not sing the carols chosen for the concert, she could not be in it at all. Such a pronouncement to a girl who loved all music as Verity-Ann did hit very hard home, and she wept saltily that night till she fell asleep. When she went into school next day, her own form loaded her with reproaches for spoiling the fun of the lesson; and when Miss Linton came back later in the week, and heard what had been happening, she spoke very seriously to her small pupil about her rudeness to Mr. Denny, and also the disgrace she had brought on her form and its form-mistress by her disobedience and discourtesy.

Verity-Ann listened to her strictures with an air of becoming meekness. Inwardly, she was no nearer doing as they wished. The rest of the school could do as they liked. Verity-Ann Carey was too patriotic to sing *German*, and even if they punished her every day of the term, *she would not do it*!

141

CHAPTER THIRTEEN

COMMANDER CAREY SOLVES THE PROBLEM

MATRON talked; Miss Burnett talked; Miss Annersley talked. For all the impression anyone made on Verity-Ann, they might just as well have saved their breath. She listened to all they had to say with the grave politeness that was so much a part of her, and then shook her small golden head.

'I'm sorry, but I'm 'fraid I can't do it. You see, I *said* I wouldn't, and I won't.'

'To think,' said Miss Burnett despairingly later on in the staff-room, 'that that – wax doll of a child should be so utterly obstinate!'

'I'll have a shot, shall I?' offered Miss Linton.

Mary Burnett laughed with an affectionate glance at her chum. 'You can try if you like. But when even the Abbess couldn't move her, I doubt if you could.'

'Leave it to her own clan,' advised Miss Slater, lifting her head for a moment from Upper Fourth's algebra. 'Their comments are much more likely to take effect than anything *we* could say. And they'll be much franker, too.'

But though the Upper Second were pitilessly blunt in expressing their views on her behaviour, Verity-Ann was not to be persuaded into changing her mind.

'I have said I won't sing anything by any German,' she informed them, 'and I mean it. Don't *you* mean what you say when you say anything?'

'Yes; but we wouldn't be such idiots as to say a silly thing like that,' said Doris Hill. 'I s'pose you won't learn any of their piano music either, then? Well, you're a goat!'

'I have a right to my own opinion,' retorted Verity-Ann.

'Yes; and Plato has a right to his!' This was Vi Lucy. 'You know what he's said – he won't let you join in any-

142

thing for the concert unless you back down and tell him you're sorry, and will sing that carol and any others he likes to give you. You'll miss all the fun of the concert, 'cos I don't suppose they'll let you even go if you're not in it *at all*. Oh, Verity-Ann! How can you be such a – such a *ninny*?'

In despair, Verity-Ann turned from them. 'I'm not going to do it!' she said. 'You can call me all the names you like, and be just as horrid as you like, but you won't make me change! So there!'

Mary-Lou, who had been sitting on top of her desk, slipped down and ran after her as she marched out of the room, her hands clenched at her sides, her lips set in an effort to keep them from quivering.

Mary-Lou caught up with Verity-Ann and slipped an arm round her shoulders. Verity-Ann shook her off, but Mary-Lou was nothing daunted. She caught hold of an arm, and forced this queer little friend of hers to stop.

'Verity-Ann, *why* won't you sing any carols or songs by Germans?' she asked imploringly. 'Anyhow, old Bach hadn't anything to do with the war. He was dead ages and ages ago.'

'He was a German, though,' said Verity-Ann, coming perforce to a full stop. 'It's no good talking, Mary-Lou. I just won't. I've said it.'

'Yes; but you say lots of things all the time,' persisted Mary-Lou. 'We all do. But we don't stick to them when it's making everyone mad with us just because we've said them.'

'*I* do!'

'But honestly, Verity-Ann, I don't see why.'

'I don't suppose you do.' Verity-Ann's head was high, but tears were not very far away. In the most secret part of her heart she was very fond of Mary-Lou, who was so utterly unlike herself. She wanted badly to please her; but having once made her stand, she was far too proud to own herself in the wrong and give in. 'I suppose Mary-Lou will never be chums with me now,' she thought desolately.

143

Mary-Lou released her arm, and stood staring at her in honest puzzlement. 'You're a queer kid,' she said at last.

'I'm no more a kid than you,' retorted Verity-Ann heatedly. 'Anyhow, we're breaking rules, talking here. I'm going.' And off she went, leaving a bewildered Mary-Lou to turn round and go back to their form-room.

'Any luck?' asked Doris.

Mary-Lou shook her head despondently. 'No; I don't be'lieve the King himself could make her do it. I don't know what to do. It'll be horrid if she's out of all the fun – the only one.'

'It'll be her own silly fault,' declared Josette.

'Won't that make it horrider for her?'

'I don't know. I s'pose it might. I'll tell you, Mary-Lou!' as a bright idea struck her. 'Auntie Jo will be coming up some time this week. She hasn't been up for ages. We'll ask *her*. *She* may be able to do something about it.'

'Good idea!' Mary-Lou was firmly convinced that Jo Maynard could work miracles if she tried. 'We'll look out for her coming, and ask her. And I'm going to ask Clem in bed to-night. She may have an idea or so.'

'You can ask the whole world, but I'm certain no one can make Verity-Ann do a thing she doesn't want to!' declared Vi ungrammatically. 'Oh, bother! There's the bell for prep and I haven't got a thing ready! Mind out, Doris! I want to get at my locker!'

As most of the Upper Second were in the same state as Vi, there was a general rush for the lockers, and when Jacynth Hardy arrived to take their prep, she opened the door on a pushing, scrimmaging herd of small girls at the lockers, while Verity-Ann, who had had everything ready before she left the room, sat in solitary state at her desk, writing out her spelling mistakes in Dictée.

'Have you taken leave of your senses, all of you!' demanded the indignant prefect when she had gained silence by the simple means of marching up to the mistress's desk and thumping on it with a clenched fist. 'Go to your seats at once, all of you! What do you mean by behaving like this?'

They slunk to their seats with full arms, and sat down, aware that they were in for a well-deserved 'wigging'. They got it. Jacynth was a quiet person as a rule, but on this occasion she was fully roused, and by the time she had finished giving Upper Second A her unvarnished opinion of them, they were all subdued enough. She finally condemned them to losing a good conduct mark each, and also – which they felt far more – to writing out in their best handwriting 'I must not be unprepared for preparation again' in English, French, and German, ten times in each language. As this had to be done before they could do any homework, most of them realized that there would be trouble on the morrow, for at their age 'best' handwriting is a slow affair, and thirty lines of it – besides working it out into good French and German – would take some time. They tried to protest, but Jacynth was adamant. Those lines had to be done and handed in to her before a single book was opened. Feeling very sorry for themselves, they set to work, and then when the lines had been passed, turned to preparation with a vim not often found among them. Jacynth, glancing up from her own French essay, smiled grimly at their absorption. But she said nothing until preparation came to an end. Then she added the finishing touch to their dismay.

'After supper, every girl will come back here and make up the prep time she has missed over those lines. I'll come with you, for I've noted down the time each set was handed in, so I know just when you ought to go. Leave books in tidy piles on your desks, and go and wash your hands for supper. And don't let me have to send for anyone, either. Verity-Ann Carey is the only girl who will *not* come back.' Then, gathering together her own books, she stalked forth, leaving them to obey her.

It is on record that, for the rest of that term at any rate, preparation bell found Upper Second A ready and sitting in their seats when the prefect on duty appeared.

'Quite an idea of yours, Jacynth,' said Gillian Culver approvingly. 'It's quite a treat to have *one* form that will be waiting and ready when one goes to them. We might try it on with some of the others.'

But that was later. That night, when Clem came up to bed, she found a Mary-Lou who was waiting to pour out all her woes to her. She listened in silence to Jacynth's treatment of them, but she shook her head when the young lady finally left that subject and went on to Verity-Ann.

'I don't see that you can do anything more. The more you talk, the worse she'll be. Oh, talk to Mrs. Maynard, by all means. But I doubt if even *she* can do anything much about it.'

'I b'lieve there's *one* person who could,' said Mary-Lou with a sudden flash of insight.

'Who's that? Better turn them on to the little moke.'

'I can't! It's her father, and I don't know where he is.'

'Then you've rather had it, haven't you? But I do agree there. I should think Verity-Ann would listen to *him* all right.'

'I know. But I don't even know if he's in England. And meantime she's out of all the fun, and everyone is so fearfully down on us just 'cos she's being such a moke and she's in our form,' wailed Mary-Lou.

'Rot! No one is going to blame your crowd for what Verity-Ann does. She's awfully like "the-Cat-That-Walked" – likes to be on her own, and do things alone, I mean. To-night's riot was your own silly faults,' Clem told her bracingly. 'There's the lights-out bell so we'll have to stop talking. Good night, old thing. Don't worry about Verity-Ann. She's a queer little object. I don't suppose she minds so fearfully much being out of things – not as *you* would, for instance. Now pipe down and go to sleep. I'm going to turn the light off.'

Mary-Lou did as she was told, and silence reigned. But Clem, far-seeing girl as she was, was wrong about Verity-Ann. That small person *did* care; and when everyone else in Junior school was fast asleep – even Mary-Lou, who had lain awake longer than usual worrying – Verity-Ann was lying sobbing as noiselessly as she could into her pillow. She just *couldn't* give in, and yet if she didn't she would be out of all the fun, and also, so far as she could see, not only out of the concert, but out of all the school fun for the rest of her time at the Chalet School, for the others would certainly never want her when they all felt she was disgracing the form as she was doing. Even Mary-Lou wouldn't want her, and she *had* been kind and much more friendly than the others. At this point, Verity-Ann nearly betrayed herself by a loud gulp. Luckily, it disturbed no one, and in the shock of fear lest anyone should come and catch her crying, she contrived to get hold of herself, and fell asleep at last.

They had another singing lesson next day, and Miss Linton, before it began, called Verity-Ann alone into the staff-room, and tried to reason with her. All to no purpose! Verity-Ann remained as polite as ever, but she flatly refused to sing any Bach or any other German music. Finally, Miss Linton sent her away with the remark, 'Well, you know what it means. You will be out of everything, and you will be the first Chalet School girl to whom *that* has happened. However, if you won't obey, you must take your punishment. Go to Matron, and she will give you a sheet to hem. But I am very sorry, and very disappointed with you, Verity-Ann. You are spoiling all my pleasure of having your form. And what is more, you are spoiling the pleasure of the others. Don't you think you are being very selfish?'

She said no more, and Verity-Ann trailed off to find Matron, who was none too pleased at having to oversee her sewing, and spoke her mind freely and to the point. Verity-Ann took it all with meekness; but once more she cried herself to sleep that night. She hadn't liked Miss Linton's remarks about being selfish and spoiling other people's pleasure. Besides, in common with the rest of the form, she 'adored' the pretty, young mistress who was such a good sort. Not that Verity-Ann would have phrased it

147

like that herself. What she thought was that she really liked Miss Linton very much, and she was miserable, thinking like that herself. What she thought was that she really liked in her form.

'But I've *said* I won't do it, and I *can't* do it, she thought.

It was nearly the end of the week before Jo Maynard managed to get up to the school, where she was welcomed thankfully by Miss Annersley, who was as much at her wits' end over Verity-Ann as anyone, and who hoped that Jo might manage to make the small girl see sense.

'I'll do my best,' said Jo, relinquishing her baby to the Head, 'but I doubt if I can make much difference when none of the rest of you has managed it.'

Verity-Ann was sent for, and the Head departed with Michael to show him off to Matron and such of the staff as she could find, while Jo, alone with Verity-Ann, tried to get her to see reason. As she had said, it was in vain. The small girl was quite polite, and quite determined. Jo explained to her painstakingly what Plato had meant by saying that all genius is extra-territorial, and that its gift is not to any one country but to the whole world. She found out that Verity-Ann had been brought up on Greek myth and legend, and pointed out that if Homer had been confined to Greece, little English girls could never have enjoyed his tales. It was no use. Verity-Ann merely looked politely interested, and said nothing. Finally, the lady produced her last shot.

'Your Daddy is coming home soon, Verity-Ann. What do you think he will say about your conduct?'

Verity-Ann flushed, but she said nothing, and Jo, utterly baffled, got up from her chair, remarking, 'Well, I see you intend to be silly and obstinate, and make yourself and other people miserable, just to save your own pride. I shan't waste any more breath on you. You'd better run back to whatever it is you ought to be doing now. Ask your form-mistress if she will excuse Mary-Lou for a few moments.'

Verity-Ann went, and Mary-Lou came two minutes later to fling herself into the arms outstretched to catch her and cry,' Auntie Jo, have you done anything about Verity-Ann? 'Cos the little moke is being horridly miserubble, and *we* can't do anything, though we've all tried our very hardest.'

'I've tried, but she won't listen. I think perhaps all you people going for her as stiffened her and made her resolve not to give in whatever happens,' said Jo. 'Can you get the rest of your crowd to stop it, Mary-Lou? Ask them to say no more about it to her, will you? You can say I asked you, if you like. Now tell me; I haven't seen Mother for a few days: Do you know if she's heard anything more about Commander Carey?'

'Yes; I had a letter this morning, and she said he was in this country in hospital. Oh, Auntie Jo! Do you think *he* could do anything about it? But he's in Scotland. Would they let Verity-Ann go to him there?'

'Does she know where he is?' asked Jo, ignoring the eager question. 'Has he written to her?'

'I know she's had no letters, 'cos when I got Mother's, she said how much she wished *she* had someone to write to her – not just an old lawyer. And Mother said I wasn't to say anything about it yet, so I haven't. I haven't told anyone but you. '

'Good! Well, I must see my girls now, and then Michael and I must get home before it's dark. No; you can't see him to-day. Miss Annersley went off with him, and I don't know just where she is. You run back into lessons. And, Mary-Lou – be extra kind to Verity-Ann. I think you're quite right in saying that she's miserable. See if you can't cheer her up a little. Going to get that form promotion, do you think?'

'I don't know. I'm working as hard as I can, and I've never been lower than third since half-term, so I'm hoping. So's Vi and Doris. Jo says they'll never let her go up, 'cos she's young for our form, anyhow. But us three may have a chance.'

'They certainly won't let Josette go up,' said that young
149

lady's aunt decidedly. 'I hope you three manage your remove, though. Now, will you go and ask if my girls can be excused to see me for a few minutes? And then I must collect Michael and go. Good-bye, pet. Be a good girl, and do what you can to help Verity-Ann.'

She kissed Mary-Lou, and then let her go, and Mary-Lou departed at full speed. Jo sat waiting for her own small fry, and a smile lit up her black eyes as she thought of Mary-Lou, such a very ordinary little schoolgirl, and so very normal. Even her funny little ways were just those that the average child would have picked up through being always with older people. Verity-Ann was a cat of another colour. However, by this time Mrs. Maynard had made up her mind what to do, and when she had spent a quarter of an hour with her triplets and sent them back to work again, she rose, left the room, and set off to hunt for the Head, and her son with a tranquil heart.

'What luck, Joey?' asked Miss Annersley when she was run to earth in the little sitting-room she shared with Miss Wilson, her co-head and the science mistress. 'Have you managed to show her the error of her ways, or is she still adamant?'

'Oh, granite personified,' said Jo cheerfully as she took her baby. 'Hello, Nell! Haven't seen you for ages. What about coming down to tea on Sunday, both of you?'

The two looked at each other. Finally, Miss Annersley nodded. 'We will. Many thanks, Joey. On the whole, it'll be a relief to get away from school for a few hours. Thank goodness the holidays begin in less than a fortnight now! But what about Verity-Ann?'

'Oh, *I* had no success. I told you I shouldn't. But I think I've got an idea which will solve the difficulty,' said Jo mysteriously as she tucked Michael back into the Moses' ark.

'What is it?' demanded Miss Wilson.

'We'll wait and see if it comes off. I think it may just turn the scale, but I'm saying nothing till I know. I mightn't be able to manage it, anyhow. It all depends.'

And with this dark and sibylline saying, Jo gathered up her son and went home.

Mary-Lou duly gave Upper Second A Mrs. Maynard's message, and most of them agreed that she might be right, and they had better abstain from teasing Verity-Ann any further. The only two dissidents were a twelve-year-old, Margaret Jones by name, who was inclined to be rough, and to take the shortest path to getting what she wanted, and Phil Craven who might be likely to prove a maths genius in years to come, but who never lost a chance of arguing. However, Vi, catching Margaret scolding Verity-Ann in a corner in her most bullying manner, made short work of her.

'I've told you we're all to leave it alone,' she said sharply. 'We've all decided to leave it alone, and you going on at Verity-Ann like that is *bullying*, Margaret Jones, and I won't have it!'

'*You* won't have it?' jeered Margaret. 'And what business is it of yours what I say to Verity-Ann Carey, I'd like to know?'

'I'm form prefect, so it is my business. And if you don't shut up and let Verity-Ann alone, I'll jolly well report you!' retorted Vi.

Margaret had no answer to this – or none that would have done – so she contented herself with snorting and turning on her heel, and leaving the other two. Vi watched her go, and then turned to her victim.

'You come with me. I'm not going to have any bullying in the form so long as I'm its prefect,' she ordered. And later on, when Phil Craven began something about 'I do wish you'd see sense, Verity-Ann!' Doris and Mary-Lou were at hand, and what was left of Phil's assurance by the time they had done with her wasn't worth mentioning. Thereafter, the subject was taboo among them.

The week-end passed with nothing of note occurring. The two Heads went to have tea at Plas Gwyn, but Jo kept off the topic of Verity-Ann's misdemeanours, and as the Triplets were also at home, having had week-end leave, nothing could be said before them. So they brought back the small girls to school, both as wise as they had left it. But Jo seemed very pleased with herself, and they had to find what comfort they could in that.

Next day there was a carol practice in the afternoon, and Upper Second A waited with a good deal of apprehension for what would happen. True to their resolve, they said nothing to Verity-Ann herself, but the leading lights of the form got together at Break, and discussed it hurriedly. Mary-Lou then made a startling suggestion.

'Clem says, couldn't some of us go and ask Plato to let Verity-Ann come and sing all the *other* carols first and then go to Matey while the rest of us sang the German ones?' she said.

'Mary-Lou Trelawney! Are you and Clem completely crackers?' Vi demanded. 'He'd eat the lot of us!'

'He couldn't *do* very much; Mary-Lou pointed out sensibly. 'I s'pose he might rag us; but we're accustomed to that more or less.'

'What put such a mad idea into your head?' Josette demanded.

'Not what – *who*. I told you it was Clem. I told her I loathed seeing Verity-Ann so miserable,' said Mary-Lou earnestly. 'She said we couldn't do anything about it with *her*, so it might be a good idea to try the other way and see if we could do anything with Plato.'

Gasps went up at the bare idea of trying to 'do anything' with that member of the Staff.

'Do let's try it!' urged Mary-Lou. 'No one's said we mustn't, and I do so loathe seeing her look like that.'

'D'you mean for all of us to go?' Vi asked doubtfully.

'Clem said better not. She said, "Choose two or three of you – the ones he likes best if you know who those are – and see what he says." She says he's quite reasonable really. And he's had time to get over his rage. Won't you?'

'What'll you do if we don't?' asked Doris curiously.

'I don't know,' began Mary-Lou. Then her face cleared.

'Yes; I do! I'll go by myself. But I wish some of you'd come and back me up. Look here! If I swear to do all the talking, will you three come with me?'

'What are you folk gassing about?' asked Lesley Malcolm, joining them with some of the others.

They told her, and she nodded. 'I'll go with Mary-Lou if she'll have me. The rest can stick around somewhere near, and if they hear Plato going for us, they can come in and say it's all of us.'

'All right,' said Vi calmly. 'You and Mary-Lou can go; and so can Jo Russell 'cos she's one of our crowd. And I'll go 'cos I'm form prefect – oh, and Phil Craven can come 'cos she's been at Verity-Ann so much.'

Phil broke into a wild protest at this, but the rest insisted, so she subsided, and it was finally arranged that the five should wait in the corridor near the upper door of Hall for Plato, and when he came, they should ask to speak to him and then do their best for Verity-Ann. The others were to be along their own corridor, which happened to be fairly near, and be ready to come and help if he proved as awful as some people thought he would be.

'Who's going to do the talking?' asked Josette. 'Oh, I know Mary-Lou said *she* would, but it's not fair to leave it all to her. There may be a fearful row.'

'We'll take it in turns, and Mary-Lou can begin, to give us a sort of lead-off, as it was her idea first,' said Vi generously. 'There's the bell. We mustn't be late – scram, all of you!'

With one accord they 'scrammed'.

But someone else was coming who was to put an end to all the trouble before the heroic five sacrificed themselves. Half-way through the first lesson after Break, one of the maids came to summon Verity-Ann to the study, and when she finally got to the room and was making her curtsy to Miss Annersley, she stopped short. The Head was not alone. With her was a tall, dark man, thin and pale under the heavy tan of the hot sun. Verity-Ann stopped dead at sight of him, and began to tremble. As for him, he got up from his chair and held out his arms. 'Verity-Ann! My own little girl!'

Verity-Ann stared at him, unbelieving wonder in her gentian-blue eyes. Then, with a cry of 'Father! Oh, Father! I thought you would never come!' she flung her arms round his neck as he lifted her to his shoulder.

Kind Miss Annersley glanced at the pair and then slipped out, unnoticed by either of them. Nor did she go back for more than an hour. When she finally returned, it was to find a Verity-Ann who slipped off her father's knee and came to make the curtsy she had interrupted at the door.

Miss Annersley smiled, and laid her hands on the small shoulders. 'Happy now, Verity-Ann?'

'Oh, *yes*!' Verity-Ann's eyes were lustrous as no one at the Chalet School had ever seen them before. 'And please, Miss Annersley, I want to say I'm sorry about the carol. Father has explained it all to me, and I'd like to say I'm sorry to Pla – I mean Mr. Denny, and ask him to let me try again.'

'So that,' as Mary-Lou told Clem in bed that night, 'is the end of that, and it's all right. I'd have gone to Plato like you said if it hadn't been, but I'm *jolly* glad I didn't have to after all, even though the others were sports and were going to back me up.'

Clem, standing at the switch to turn off the light, nodded. 'I rather thought that would happen if you gave them a lead,' she said casually. She switched off; but before she got into bed she stood by Mary-Lou's for a moment. 'The first sport was *you*, Mary-Lou. And now,' she added briskly as she snuggled down under the bedclothes, 'let's hope Verity-Ann learns a little sense. She might be quite a decent kid if anyone took her in hand.'

CHAPTER FOURTEEN

A GOOD WIND-UP

THE trouble with Verity-Ann having been satisfactorily settled, the school, and more especially the junior part of it, prepared to give its full attention to the concert which was to end the term.

It would take place on the Wednesday afternoon of the following week, and they would break up on the Thursday. No one was keener now than Verity-Ann herself. Her father must go back to hospital for treatment, but it had been arranged that it should not be to the great Glasgow hospital where he had been first sent, but to the Sanatorium over the hills which was so closely linked up with the school. Verity-Ann was to spend her holidays at Plas Gwyn so as to be near him, and Mary-Lou, with the prospect of having so many of her chums close at hand, was as wild as any small girl brought up by Gran could be; and Verity-Ann herself was not far behind her.

'Father is going to stay at Plas Gwyn until next Friday,' she told her form. 'Then he's going to the San, but he *thinks* he'll be able to come to Plas Gwyn for Christmas. Mrs. Maynard has asked him, anyway. And he's promised me faithfully that he won't go far away again until I'm quite grown-up. So I'll have him for the next six or seven years, at least. Isn't it wonderful!'

'Wizard!' Mary-Lou said, having picked up this word, and using it on every possible occasion.

What the little girls did not know, and none of their elders intended that they should know, was that Commander Carey had suffered so much from the effects of his awful journey through the Amazonian jungle that it

155

was unlikely that he would be able to continue in the Navy. At present, he was to undergo treatment at the Sanatorium for the next six months, and after that, not even the doctors could say what was likely to happen.

His companion, Dr. O'Brien, was an even worse case, for his sight was badly affected, and he was permanently blind in one eye.

Mrs. Trelawney visited constantly at Plas Gwyn to hear all that Commander Carey could tell her about her husband. On the Sunday he went to tea at Carn Beg, and Gran thrilled proudly at what he said about her son's heroism in going to try to help his comrades when he might have escaped if he had not done so.

Mary-Lou heard all about it later; at present she was too full of school affairs to think about anything else. For one thing, they were in the thick of the end-of-term exams, and she was striving tooth and nail to beat Vi Lucy and Doris Hill. For another, Miss Linton had learned during the term that she could speak verse beautifully, and she had to say a short Christmas poem that Miss Annersley had unearthed in a quaint old collection. So, what with one thing and another, she was a very busy little person for the whole week. But when Saturday came, the poem was safely in her memory; exams were over, and if she didn't get her remove, well, she could do no more about it now. She very wisely put the whole thing out of her head, and with Clem and Verity-Ann began to plan for the holidays.

Monday came but school was, to all intents and purposes, at an end. They would have a carol practice that morning, and clear up their lockers. Later, Matron would probably send for some of them to pack. Break would come at eleven, and after Break they would go to their form-rooms to hear the exam results. Mary-Lou had been hopeful during exam week itself, for she had liked most of the papers. But just now she felt gloomily certain that she had done badly, and would be half-way down the form, and there would be no chance of a remove.

Clem, who had not worried at all over her work, taking it more or less in her stride, was free from such fears. She neither expected nor wanted a remove. She was very happy where she was, and quite content to stay there for the next two terms. As for the others, Vi and Lesley were a prey to the same fears as Mary-Lou, and Josette was openly hoping and praying that no one would be sent up. Doris, who had done her honest best, was willing to wait for the lists, and did her best to cheer up her despondent chums.

'If one of us gets a move, most likely all four of us will,' she said to Mary-Lou when they were alone together for a few minutes. 'And if we don't, we'll be together, anyhow. The only thing I hope is that whatever happens we do stick together. There's the bell for the prac! Come on, Mary-Lou; and do stop looking like a funeral!'

The practice went with a swing. The girls knew the carols thoroughly now, and enjoyed them. The recitations and dances were good, and Mary-Lou's grave little-girl voice repeating Henry Vaughan's 'On Christ's Nativity' was to be heard all over the hall.

'You aren't half-bad, Mary-Lou,' said Vi as they went to seek their milk and biscuits. 'And I do love that funny poem of yours.'

'I rather love it myself,' Mary-Lou conceded.

Elevenses over, they went to their form-room, and for once they settled at their desks at once, and waited for Miss Linton to finish her coffee and come. It seemed a long wait, but she arrived at last, a bunch of slips in her hand. Phil Craven shut the door, and returned to her seat, and when they had all sat down, the young mistress proceeded to read out the lists.

Most of the subjects had gone as was to be expected. Phil was top in arithmetic. Vi and Doris had tied in geography, with Mary-Lou and Josette close behind. Angela Carter, one of the twins, headed the grammar list, and Anne, the other one, evened things up by coming second in New Testament, which Mary-Lou headed. Mary-Lou was also top in French and Latin, and second in German, of which Vi was head. Lesley obtained a good all-round showing, and Doris had also done well.

At last all the subject lists had been read – even Miss Davidson's art list, where Verity-Ann was bottom. Indeed, she had not shone anywhere. Mary-Lou beat her hollow in most subjects, and as for Josette, baby of the form as she was, she was never lower in any subject than sixth. Miss Linton took up her last sheet, and there was an excited stir among the twenty-odd small girls in the room.

Miss Linton smiled at them. 'I am very proud of my form,' she said. 'You have gained the highest average form mark in the school. I know that this is partly owing to a few of you who have set the standard for work. I hope that when next term comes, and the five people who head the list – three top, and two next – are in Lower Third, those of you left behind will carry on their standard. Now for the form list!' And she began to read: 'Top, Doris Hill, Vi Lucy and Mary-Lou Trelawney; next, Lesley Malcolm and Ruth Barnes; next, Josette Russell – Angela Carter – Josefa Wertheim — '

She went on, but Mary-Lou heard no more. She was actually top – tied with Vi and Doris! How pleased Mother and Gran would be! And, more than that, she had won her coveted remove. Life at that moment could hold no more for Mary-Lou!

She roused up when, the lists ended, the rest began to chatter, and she saw Verity-Ann with a very mournful face turning to her. 'Oh, Mary-Lou! We shan't be in the same form any more!'

'Where were you 'zackly?' Mary-Lou asked.

'Nineteenth. It's awfully low, isn't it! I do feel sick about it!'

Mary-Lou could scarcely believe her ears. Verity-Ann talking slang! 'I do b'lieve you'll be just like one of us by this time next year,' she said slowly.

Verity-Ann's face flushed, and her eyes shone. 'Do you really mean that, Mary-Lou?' she asked shyly. 'Father *said* he'd like me to be more – more like girls are to-day.'

'Then you'll do it all right,' said Mary-Lou confidently. 'Yes, Jacynth; I'm coming – I'm coming *now*!' And she fled at Jacynth's summons to do her packing.

After that, the concert next day was almost an anti-climax, even though Tony was there with Mother and Mr. Young and Commander Carey. When it was over, and audience and performers were mingling at what Clem called 'a stand-up tea', Tony tugged at Mary-Lou's pig-tails, and she promptly retorted with an onslaught on his cropped locks.

'You leave my hair alone!' she ordered.

'I just wanted to see if you'd grown prim,' he explained. 'School so often makes such ninnies of girls.'

'And don't *you* talk like that, either,' added Clem, who was standing near. 'Why,' accusingly, 'you look quite decent! Even your parting's straight and your nails are clean!'

'And your hair is shiny,' riposted Tony, 'and your blouse is clean, and you had a decent hanky just now. Mary-Lou always did look a lot cleaner than us – except when we'd all been messing about on the shore. But *you*! And swanky bows on your hair! Still,' he added magnani-mously, 'I must say it doesn't seem to have done you any harm. It must be quite a decent place for a girls' school!'

'It's the Chalet School,' said Verity-Ann's silvery little voice as she came up to them, and tucked her hand through Mary-Lou's arm.

'I should think it *was* decent!' cried Mary-Lou in-dignantly. 'It's the jolliest school in the world!'

'Hear! hear!' said Clem.

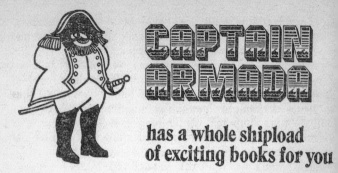

CAPTAIN ARMADA

has a whole shipload of exciting books for you

Armadas are chosen by children all over the world. They're designed to fit your pocket, and your pocket money too – and they make terrific presents for friends. They're colourful, exciting, and there are hundreds of titles to choose from – thrilling mysteries, spooky ghost stories, hilarious joke books, brain-teasing quizzes and puzzles, fascinating hobby books, stories about ponies and schools – and many, many more. Armada has something for everyone.

Book Tokens

Give them
the pleasure of choosing
Book Tokens can be bought
and exchanged at most
bookshops.

Armada